SWAMI VIVEKANANDA
AND
INDIAN SOCIETY

MJP
PUBLISHERS

SWAMI VIVEKANANDA *AND* INDIAN SOCIETY

S. Babu

Head of the Department
Department of History
Kanchi Mamunivar Centre for Post-Graduate Studies
(Autonomous), Pondicherry

Chennai   New Delhi   Tirunelveli

ISBN 978-81-8094-296-9   **MJP Publishers**

No. 44 Nallathambi Street,
Triplicane,
Chennai 600 005

MJP 250

Publisher : C. Janarthanan

≋ Foreward ≋

Swami Vivekananda was the first Indian to call in question the superiority of the West and to assert the spiritual pre-eminence and incomparable greatness of India instead of defending his religion against the attacks of its critics. He attempted at the spiritual conquest of the world while the European powers strove for the political and economic subjugation of India. The monks of the Mission founded by him engaged themselves in the service of humanity by alleviating suffering, providing medical aid to the sick and looking after the orphans as well as imparting education through setting up schools and other institutions. He emphatically taught that salvation does not come through the life of a recluse, but by serving God in man. He did not believe in social reform programme that catered to an elitist group. He argued that education, with all that it implied, would automatically rid society of its ailments, thereby dispensing with the necessity of a formal movement.

I am immensely happy that the Department of History, Kanchi Mamunivar Centre for Post-Graduate Studies, Puducherry has honoured Swami Vivekananda on his **Sesquicentennial Birth Anniversary** by organising a national seminar coordinated by Dr. S. Babu. It is further noted that some of the selected papers of the seminar are brought out in the form of a book to disseminate widely the ideals of Swami Vivekananda and the spirit of his Mission.Various aspects of Swamiji's message to humanity at large and to the different sections of the Indian society in particular and also the relevance of his teachings to the contemporary milieu as the guiding principles to the youth on the whole are dealt with in detail. It is hoped that the noble ideals of Swami Vivekananda, through this publication, will definitely reach out to the young generation and inspire them in the right direction.

Prof. K.S. Mathew

Director
Institute for Research in Social Sciences and Humanities
Nirmalagiri P.O, Kannur Dt. Kerala.

✑ Preface ✑

This collection of essays is the outcome of a National seminar on **"Social Changes in India and Swami Vivekananda (1863-1920) on his sesquicentennial** birth anniversary held in the Department of History, Kanchi Mamunivar Centre for Post-Graduate Studies, Pondicherry, on 10-11 January, 2013. The present collection represents a small beginning in the direction as an inspiration from the life and teachings of Swami Vivekananda as a guiding principle to the youth of India and the humanity as a whole. In a short span of life, Swamiji immensely contributed to arousing his countrymen not only against foreign rule but also for making a better world wherein all could live happily and in harmony without any discrimination and exploitation. Swamiji was a man of enormous mental strength and determination. He is considered to have inspired India's freedom struggle and also considered as the "maker of modern India". His varied ideas and thoughts on India and its people were brought out by the scholars from different parts of India. All the papers in the volume throw great light on the on the perceptions and ideas of Swamiji.

The seminar was sponsored by the Indian Council of Historical Research and the University Grants Commission, New Delhi. I am very much grateful to the ICHR and the UGC for taking a great deal of interest in funding the seminar.

I am also grateful to the Director of our centre and to all my colleagues in the Department for rendering a great service in the successful completion of the seminar. I am immensely thankful to my wife and children who made me from the domestic chores and extended their full cooperation in the success of the seminar.

I am greatly obliged to Prof. K.S. Mathew, the founder Head of the Department of History, Pondicherry University, Pondicherry and currently Director, Institute for Research in Social Sciences and Humanities, Nirmalagiri, Kerala, for taking pains to go through the pages of this work and writing a Foreword.

I am beholden to express my sincere thanks to M/S. MJP Publishers the publishers for publishing the volume expeditiously well.

Contents

– Contents –

Chapter 1

Swami Vivekananda and the Concept of Harmony of Religions

Jose C. C.

Department of History
Christ University
Bangalore

Model of power and power of model are two concepts by which we understand nations and their strengths. Many nations today are known for their model of power either with their military might or economic power. The pages of history give us the best stories of how the powerful countries have retained their position of influence and even declined while focusing on these strengths. India has the power of model of harmony and co-existence of religions as highlighted by Swami Vivekananda in the World Parliament of Religions in Chicago. Uniqueness of Indian model is evident from the ever embracing attitude of welcoming different faiths to its land over the centuries. He mentions the presence and co-existence of Hebrews, Jews, Persians and Christians for many centuries in the land of India as the clear proof for the same.[1] Swami Vivekananda got inspired by the edict of Asoka the great and tried to base his arguments for

---

[1] *The Complete Works of Swami Vivekananda*, Vol. I, 2003, p. 391.

religious harmony on that, "one should not exalt one's own sect and decry others, but tender them on every occasion the honour they deserve... Whosoever, from attachment to his own sect and with a view to promoting it, decries others, only deals rude blows to his own sect. All people should be encouraged to promote the essential moral doctrines in each and mutual respects for all the other sects"[2].

The importance of harmony among religions was highlighted by Swami Vivekananda by focusing on its long lasting impact of bringing peace and progress of the world.[3] In fact looking at the betterment of humanity, hate will bring more negative results in the nation as a whole and even among individual human beings. The significance of harmony among religions was brought forward by him focusing on positive values like mutual regard, friendliness and cooperation as against the negative values of bigotry, intolerance, narrowness and sectarianism.[4]

Concept of Religion

The three parts of religion which Swami Vivekananda tried to explain started with the philosophy which contained the scope and basic principles of religion, the goal and the means of attaining it.[5] The mythology which includes the legends of the men connected with it, the supernatural beings is the second part.[6] Here the imaginary lives of men and its supernatural beings are represented to make the philosophy of the religion more concrete. Rituals, the most expressive part of the religion, forms the third part.[7] Forms and ceremonies, various physical attitudes and flowers and incense are part of it. Since most of the recognized religions exist on these elements but give emphasis differently, an understanding of these give us the idea that different religions give stress on different aspects.

---

2   Ibid, Vol. VII, P. 288.
3   Ajeet Jawed, *Swami Vivekananda, An Iconoclastic Ascetic*, New Delhi, 2007, p. 85.
4   Ibid, p. 89.
5   *The Complete Works of Swami Vivekananda*, Vol. II, op. cit., p. 377.
6   Ibid, p. 377.
7   Ibid, p. 377.

According to him, "religion is not in doctrines, in dogmas, nor in intellectual augmentation; it is being and becoming, it is realization".[8]

His concept of religion was more practical than what existed in theory. Bringing forward a practical concept of religion, he highlighted the gist of religion as 'to be good and to do good'. From this point he brought in the true message of religion as the idea of unity with its expressions of hope and cheer. Stressing on the underlying unity among religions, he tried to give focus on the essential aspect of religion as love of God and love of man.[9] A basic concept on which he wanted a person to be member of a religion is freedom.[10] According to him it should be left to the choice of the individual. Disapproving the compulsions, he was even against the parents imposing their religion upon their children.[11] Here he was suggesting a person selecting the best according to one's wish, *ishta*, and preserving the same. In this sense he was against the practice of indoctrination.

Another basic nature of religion which Swami Vivekananda proposed was its inclusive nature. It includes having a broader understanding of other religions and their followers.[12] It is in this context that he asked his followers "to become broad, to go out, to amalgamate, to universalize..."[13].

The idea of unity was presented by Swami Vivekananda as the true message of religion. The infinite oneness of the soul is the base on which the spiritual oneness of the whole universe is based.[14] One of the graceful aspect of his views on religion is that of a religion of hope and cheer.[15] To an extent this view also takes care of the fruits of religion wherein one's religion need to bring hope and joy in one's own life as well as the life of others too.

---

8   Ibid, p. 43.
9   Ibid, p. 197.
10   Ajeet Jawed, *op. cit.*, p. 83.
11   Ibid, p. 84.
12   Ibid, p. 85.
13   *The Complete Works of Swami Vivekananda*, Vol. III, 1948, p. 271.
14   Ajeet Jawed, *op. cit*, p. 105.
15   Ibid, p. 82.

He also brought out the idea that since religion belongs to the soul, the language of the soul is one.[16] It is to the soul that the points of similarity and unity of religions belong to.

The World of Disharmony

Elements of both harmony and disharmony are found in different parts of the world, especially through and by religions. According to Swami Vivekananda, the forces working against harmony are sectarianism, rigidity, orthodoxy, bigotry, fanaticism, organized religions, etc. All these negative traits in fact have done more harm to humanity in general. It was his view that religion had given humanity both "the intensest love" and "the most diabolical hatred".

Swami Vivekananda was not against sects but he was against the evil effects of sects.[17] The sects are there to exist due to the understanding of truth in different ways which shows the diversity in thinking and expression. But it is the jealousy and hatred among different sects that brings disharmony in the religion and among religions. These negative effects also brings dishonor to the land of India, which is the birthplace and nurturing ground for all the sects.[18] He tried to trace the origin of different sects from the need of satisfying the hankering and the thirst of different classes of human minds.[19]

Mostly it is the selfishness that brought narrowness and brutality among religions. Self-interests of each religion posed block for other religions. According to Swami Vivekananda, this is mostly found among organized religions. So he was against organized religions and people becoming members of it. Fanaticism, which he considered as a disease of the human brain, is the most dangerous of all diseases.[20] Claiming that more harm was done by religions than good, he tried to trace the origin of it, in the narrow approaches and the limitations of religions.[21]

16   K. P. Aleaz, *Harmony of Religions, The Relevance of Swami Vivekananda*, Calcutta, 1993, p. 64.
17   Ajeet Jawed, *op. cit*, p. 82.
18   Ibid, p. 82.
19   *The Complete Works of Swami Vivekananda*, Vol. III, *op. cit.*, p. 262.
20   Ibid, Vol. II, p. 377.
21   Ibid, p. 68

It was also his belief that religious labels also contributed to disharmony among the people because they resulted in narrowness leading to dissensions among religions and religious groups.[22] The unique and distinct profile of religions was developed over the centuries.

Promotion of Harmony

1. Approaches to the Problem

The problem of harmony can be taken up from four approaches of political, social, theological and mystical. If political approach refers to the policy taken up by the government towards religion, the social approach is what is followed by common people; interpreting doctrines in favour of harmony is the theological approach and mystical experience is the direct experience of the Ultimate Reality.

2. Inter-Religious Attitudes

A person's attitude towards one's own religion and other religions were termed as exclusivism, inclusivism and pluralism by some western scholars. Swami Vivekananda contributed universalism as the fourth attitude[23] meaning there exists a set of universally valid religious principles common to or unifying all religions.

Exclusivism as the name itself suggests is all about the attitude that one's own religion is the best and true and naturally other religions are false. Extreme forms of exclusivism leads to fundamentalism.[24] The latest terrorist and extremist activities are the results of fundamentalism which threatened harmony among nations, religions and communities.

Inclusivism although had the view point of holding one's religion as true but was considering others sharing in the perfection and truth of this religion.[25] In one way inclusivism is an attitude of justi-

---

22   Ajeet Jawed, *op. cit.*, p. 105.
23   Swami Bhajanananda, Harmony of Religions from the Standpoint of Sri Ramakrishna and Swami Vivekananda – II, *Bulletin of the Ramakrishna Mission Institute of Culture*, 2012, p. 410.
24   Ibid, p. 405.
25   Ibid, p. 405.

fying and proclaiming one's own goodness and truth but on the other side it tried to appreciate the goodness and positive values in other religions as related to the religion which is inclusive.

Taking clue from the ideas of Arnold Toynbee, W. E. Hocking, and Ernst Troeltsch, pluralism is an approach of accepting the diversity in religions from the standpoint of existence of elements of truth being present in different religions.[26] The idea of pluralism is more relevant to India from the context of a multi-religious society to bring harmony among religious communities. Pluralistic thought gained momentum as religions occupy privileged, autonomous and interactive positions as per this idea.[27]

By bringing the idea of universalism, Swami Vivekananda was trying to promote the thread of unity among religions by looking at the unifying elements. In the present world scenario, which is threatened by religious fanaticism, the relevance of universalism is most important.

3. Inclusiveness

Promoting interchange of ideas and accepting of differences, he called upon religions to be inclusive with a broader outlook towards other religions. Condemning all these forces, Swami Vivekananda declared that understanding the differences among religions can be the starting point of harmony of religions.

4. Harmony and Toleration

Terming harmony as distinct from toleration, Swami Vivekananda focused on the need for inter-religious and intra-religious harmony. He was not at all accepting the term toleration as it meant that others are not correct and one accepts other's weaknesses and shortcomings and allow them to live.[28] Terming the term toleration as blasphemy, he ridiculed the approach of 'let live' out of one's mercy and consid-

---

26   Ibid, p. 406.
27   Ibid, p. 406.
28   *The Complete Works of Swami Vivekananda*, Vol. II, *op. cit.*, p. 374.

eration.[29] He was more comfortable with the term acceptance and expressed his willingness to enter any places of worship.[30]

5. Understand and Accept Differences

One of the root causes for the disharmony among religions, is that of differences among them. But Swami Vivekananda tried to bring a practical understanding of the same by claiming that these differences are just differences of expression.[31] The ignorance will be eliminated with a proper understanding of differences. He claimed, "the difference between weakness and strength is one of degree; the difference between virtue and vice is one of degree; the difference between heaven and hell is one of degree; the difference between life and death is one of degree; all differences in this world are of degree, and not of kind, because oneness is the secret of everything".[32] Condemning other religions and practices and looking down with contempt on others are all the result of lack of proper understanding of differences among religions and its practices.

Conclusion

The ideas of Swami Vivekananda on harmony of religions holds great importance today in the context of conflicts and fighting in the name of religion. One of the basic and most important practical suggestion which he gave for the same was broadmindedness, "all narrow, limited, fighting ideas of religion must be given up... The religious ideals of the future must embrace all that exists in the world and is good and great, and at the same time, have infinite scope for future development".[33] He called for the fullest play of religion so as to manifest the power of religion. Broadening of religion will necessarily result in religious ideas becoming universal, vast and infinite.[34] Religion, he claimed, when purified and broadened will be able to reach every part of the society as it

29   Ibid, p. 374.
30   Ibid, p. 374.
31   Ibid, p. 299.
32   Ibid, p. 299.
33   Romain Rolland, *Vivekananda and the Universal Gospel*, 1947, p. 283.
34   *The Complete Works of Swami Vivekananda*, Vol. II, *op. cit.*, p. 68.

has the power to do so.[35] A broadened religion will increase its power of good hundredfold.[36] But it has to be liberated from the places of worship, books, dogmas, ceremonials, forms and rituals and need to be a real, spiritual and universal concept which will make religion the real and living.[37] This will result in the sweet fruits of harmony, where religion becomes part of every aspect of society and will be doing more good than what was done earlier.

REFERENCES

1. Rolland, Romain. 1947. *The Life of Vivekananda and the Universal Gospel*, Almora, Advaita Ashrama.

2. Aleaz, K. P. 1993. *Harmony of Religious: The Relevance of Vivekananda*, Kolkata, Punthi Pustak.

3. Rahbar, Hansarj. 1995. *Vivekananda: The Warrior Saint*. Delhi, Farsight Publishers and Distributors.

4. Vivekananda. 1983. *The Complete Works of Swami Vivekananda*, Vol. I to VII, Kolkata, Advaita Ashrama.

5. Jawed, Ajeet. 2007. *Swami Vivekananda: An Iconoclastic Ascetic*, New Delhi, Ane Books, India.

6. Prasad, Bimal ed. 1994. *Swami Vivekananda: Selected Speeches and Writings*. New Delhi, Vikas Publishing House Pvt. Ltd.

7. Vivekananda. 1993. *My India, The India Eternal*, Kolkata, Ramakrishna Mission Institute of Culture,

---

35 Ibid, p. 68.
36 Ibid, p. 68.
37 Ibid, p. 68.

Chapter 2

Who Inspired Swami Vivekananda?

Sandeep Kumar Dasari

Associate Professor of History
Tagore Arts college
Puducherrry – 605 008.

Swami Vivekananda known as "awakener of soul", great orator, inspiring teacher, humanist, well read, propagated his views without any fear and his writings can inspire young generations on nationality, patriotism and religious tolerance. His Guru Ramakrishna Paramahamsa's views were propagated through Ramakrishna Mission as a tribute to his spiritual mentor.

His speeches at Hyderabad and Chicago and maturity for accepting greatness of all religions, made him a favourite speaker at world conference. Even national leaders were influenced by his writings and great quotations like "Take up one idea, Make that one idea your life—think of it, dream of it, and live on that idea. Let the brain, muscles, nerves, every part of your body, be full of that idea, and just leave every other idea alone. This is the way to success". He always propagated for purification of mind, true worship, atma-vikasa, self-

9

assertion and positive attitude in his words. Strength is Life; Weakness is Death. Expansion is Life; Contraction is Death. Love is life; Hatred is Death. He propagated that "Freedom can never be reached by the weak. Throw away all weakness. Tell your body that it is strong, tell your mind that it is strong and have unbounded faith and hope in yourself" and inspired millions by his great saying "Arise, awake and stop not till the goal is reached". He cleverly and wisely propagated the greatness of the Hindutva and its great spiritual values, Indian culture and Hindu Dharma.

Buddha brought the Vedanta to light, gave it to people, and saved India. A thousand years after his death ... Sankaracharaya arose and once more revived the Vedanata philosophy. He made it a rationalistic philosophy. In the Upanishads the arguments are often very obscure. By Buddha the moral side of the philosophy was laid stress upon, and by Sankaracharaya the intellectual side. He worked out, rationalised and placed before men the wonderful coherent system of Advaita.

Inspiration of Swami Vivekananda by Buddha and Christ

In every religion we find one type of self-devotion particularly developed. The type of working without a motive is most highly developed in Buddhism. Buddhism is one of our sects. It was founded by a great man called Gautama, who became disgusted at the eternal metaphysical discussions of his day, and the cumbrous rituals, and more especially with the caste system. Some people say that we are born to a certain caste and therefore we are superior to others who are not thus born. He was also against the tremendous priest craft. He preached a religion in which there was no motive power, and which was perfectly agnostic about metaphysics or theories about God. He was often asked if there was a God, and he answered, he did not know. When asked about right conduct, he would reply, "Do good and be good".

There came five Brahmins, who asked him to settle their discussion. One said, "Sir, my book says that God is such and such, and that this is the way to come to God". Another said, "That is wrong, for my book says such and such, and this is the way to come to God" and

10

so others. He listened calmly to all of them, and then asked them one by one. "Does any one of your books say that God becomes angry, that He ever injures any one, that He is impure?" "No, Sir, they all teach that God is pure and good". Then, my friends, why do you not become pure and good first, that you may know what God is? Of course I do not endorse all his philosophy. I want a good deal of metaphysics, for myself. I entirely differ in many respects, but, because I differ, is that any reason why I should not see the beauty of the man? He was the only man who was bereft of all motive power. There were other great men who all said they were the Incarnations of God Himself, and that those who would believe in them would go to heaven. But what did Buddha say with his dying breath? "None can help you; help yourself; work out your own salvation". He said about himself, "Buddha is the name of infinite knowledge, infinite as the sky; I, Gautama, have reached that state; you will all reach that too if you struggle for it". Bereft of all motive power, he did not want to go to heaven, did not want money; he gave up his throne and everything else and went about begging his bread through the streets of India, preaching for the good of men and animals with a heart as wide as the ocean.

He was the only man who was ever ready to give up his life for animals to stop sacrifice. He once said to a king, "If the sacrifice of a lamb helps you to go to heaven, sacrificing a man will help you better; so sacrifice me". The king was astonished. And yet this man was without motive of power. He stands as the perfection of the active type, and the very height to which he attained shows that through the power of work we can also attain to the highest spirituality. To many the path becomes easier if they believe in God. But the life of Buddha shows that even a man who does not believe in God, has no metaphysics, belongs to no sect, and does not go to any church, or temple, and is a confessed materialist, even he can attain to the highest. We have no right to judge him. I wish I had one infinitesimal part of Buddha's heart. Buddha may or may not have believed in God; that does not matter to me. He reached the same state of perfection to which others come by Bhakti-love of God-Yoga, or Jnana. Perfection comes through the disinterested performance of action. To the beginner, Christ would immediately speak of the Personal God: 'Pray to your Father in Heaven'. To the one a little more advanced, he would say, 'I am the vine, ye are the branches'. But to the one who was fully advanced and his dear disciple, he would proclaim: 'I and my Father are One'. We find the same truth echoed in Sri Ramakrishna's words. He disclosed to his beloved Naren (Vivekananda), 'He who is Rama, He who is Krishna, dwells at once in this body as Ramakrishna'. It is a sad fact that often the disciples of various paths misinterpret the teachings of their masters to the extent of claiming theirs as the only Master. In doing so, they bring their teachers down to the level of ordinary men. An aspirant, they claim, in spite of high achievements, counts for nothing unless and until he is prepared to give all credit to their master. What blind ignorance! If the master were an ear-witness of his disciple's utterance, he would burn with shame. On this Vivekananda says:

Suppose Jesus of Nazareth was teaching and a man came and told him, 'What you teach is beautiful. I believe that it is the way to perfection, and I am ready to follow it; but I do not want to worship you as the only begotten son of God'. What would be the answer of Jesus of Nazareth? 'Very well, brother, follow the ideal and advance in your own way. I do not care whether you give me the credit for the teaching or not ... I only teach the truth, and truth is nobody's property, nobody's patent truth. Truth is god Himself. Go forward'. But what the disciples say nowadays is, 'No matter whether you practice the teachings or not, do you give credit to the Man? If you credit the Master, you will be saved; if not there is no salvation for you'.

An interesting event took place when Vivekananda was staying at Thousand Island Park. It was a dark and rainy night. A few ladies from Detroit had travelled hundreds of miles to find him there. Having met him, one of them humbly spoke out, 'We have come to you just as we would go to Jesus if he were still on earth and ask him to teach us'. Vivekananda deeply moved and overwhelmed with humility, replied, 'If only I possessed the power of Christ to set you free now!' Vivekananda meant that our earthly achievements, however grandiose, are in no way enough to quench the ever-pinching thirst of human souls to attain to higher life. Christ's body is Christianity. Christianity embodies humility. Vivekananda's humility is the entire world's treasure. He once said: If you ask me, 'Is there God?' and I say 'Yes', you immediately ask my grounds for saying so, and poor me has to exercise all his powers to provide you with some reason. If you had come to Christ and said 'Is there any God?' he would have said, 'Yes', and if you had asked, 'Is there any proof?' he would have replied, 'Behold the Lord!'

Recent research has shown that Swami Vivekananda was much more indebted to all, especially the Brahmo Samaj, for his religious awakening than is commonly realised. It is from this contact that his warm appreciation of Christ is to be traced. It is significant that Swami Vivekananda inaugurated the Ramakrishna Mission, after his master's death, on Christmas Eve. But we touch the heart of Vivekananda's interpretation of Christ when we note three things. First, his approach to Christ was not that of a seeker but that of one who found satisfaction in philosophical-mystical Hinduism. Second, he is influenced by a certain historical scepticism, due to apparently being influenced by the Christ-myth speculation of the late nineteenth century. Third, he viewed everything at all times from the angle—Watch and pray, for the 'Kingdom of Heaven is at hand', which means, purify your mind and be ready! And that spirit never dies. You recollect that the Christians are, even in the darkest days, even in the most superstitious countries, always trying to prepare themselves, for the coming of the Lord, by trying to help others, building hospitals, and so on. So long as the Christians keep to that ideal, their religion lives.

So we find that in almost every religion these are the three primary things which we have in the worship of God—forms or symbols, names, God-men. All religions have these but you find that they want to fight with each other. One says, "My name is the only name; my form is the only form; and my God-men are the only God-men in the world; yours are simply myths". In modern times, Christian clergymen have become a little kinder, and they allow that in the older religions in which the different forms of worship were foreshadowing's of Christianity, which of course, they consider, is the only true form. God tested Himself in older times, tested His powers by getting these things into shape which culminated in Christianity. This, at least, is a great advance. Fifty years ago they would not have said even that; nothing was true except their own religion.

This idea is not limited to any religion, nation, or class of persons; people are always thinking that the only right thing to be done by others is what they themselves are doing. And it is here that the study of different religions helps us. It shows us that the same thoughts that we have been calling ours, and ours alone, were present hundreds of years ago, in others, and sometimes even in better form of expression than our own. All religions are, at bottom, alike. This is so, although the Christian church, like the Pharisee in the parable, thanks god that theirs alone is right and thinks that all other religions are wrong and in need of Christian light. Christianity must become tolerant before the world will be willing to unite with the Christian church in a common charity. God has not left Himself without a witness in any heart, and men, especially men who follow Jesus Christ, should be willing to admit this. In fact, Jesus Christ was willing to admit every good man to the family of God. It is not the man who believes a certain something, but the man who does the will of the Father in Heaven, who is right. On this basis, being right and doing right the whole world can unite.

Inspiration of Swami Vivekananda by Osho and Mohammedan

But Osho had a different opinion on Vivekananda. He says that Vivekananda is a very clever politician. If he is speaking amongst Christians, he will praise Christ. He has not the guts to criticize on any point. I cannot do that. If I see that something is wrong, I have to say it. If there is something good, I praise it, but I keep the right to criticize also. If he is speaking amongst Buddhists, he will not speak anything against Buddha or Buddhist scriptures. He created Ramakrishna Mission as a synthesis of all religions. Now, for me the very idea of synthesis of all religions is like synthesis of all lies, which will be far bigger a lie. There is no need of so many religions, all that is needed is a certain quality of religiousness, which is neither Hindu nor Mohammedan nor Christian. When you are truthful you are religious; when you are loving you are religious; when you are respectful of life you are religious.

That does not mean you are Hindu, does not mean you are a Buddhist. I want the whole world to be religious, but not a synthesis of Christianity and Judaism and Mohammedanism and Hinduism

14

and what kind of synthesis that will be? If you just conceive the idea, it will be such a hodgepodge. Mohammed says four wives are allowed: Now how you are going to synthesise with those who think that only one wife is religious, more than that is sin. So the synthesis will be two wives! Neither the Mohammedan will be ... agreeing to it nor is the non-Mohammedan going to agree. Mohammed himself married none women, naturally, he is no ordinary man. Ordinary men are marrying four; an extraordinary man, a prophet of God has to marry nine. How you are going to synthesise? Jains think unless you are naked and live naked without any possessions you cannot be enlightened. Now, according to Jains even Gautama Buddha is not enlightened, because he uses clothes. How are you going to synthesise these people?

If you ask Jains, Buddhists and Hindus that Jesus Christ crucifixion is for the salvation of humanity, that it is the greatest sacrifice God has given, His own son, to save humanity—all the three will laugh. They will say that "This is stupid! God who is omnipotent can create the whole world; He can change it any moment—without any sacrifice, without any crucifixion, without all this drama". Secondly, they cannot accept Jesus as enlightened, because he is being crucified. According to Hindus, Jains and Buddhists—all the religions born in India—anybody who is enlightened cannot be crucified. Existence is not so unkind. Of course, in India it has never happened. I am not saying they are right: only I am saying how you are going to compromise all these people? It will be a bazaar, and everybody disagreeing on every point. Mohammedans say God created animals for man to eat—no question of argument, because it is written in the book of God and the book of God cannot be questioned. One of the jailers in America, a very educated man, came to give me a Bible seeing that I am just sitting the whole day with closed eyes, doing nothing—good chance to convert a man. So he gave me a Bible. He said, "This is the book of God".

I said, "If it is a book of God, then certainly I will keep it with respectfully, but how did you come to know? When God told you?"

He said, "No, God has not told me, it is written in the book".

I said, "You are educated, intelligent...I can write a book and can write it: These are the words of God. Will you believe that book, that it is words of God?"

He said, "No".

"But then why you can believe Jesus' words? What is the difference in my words and Jesus' words to you? And if this is the book of God, then what about Koran?—The same claim ... What about Vedas, the same claim; what about Gita, the same claim. So Ramakrishna Mission is a political movement, trying to be nice to everyone. So everybody is right, everybody is good. And don't bring any controversial things in—just compare those things which can be compared without any controversy. That's why they are not opposed".

My situation is just the opposite: I don't believe that any of the organized religion is worth saving. They are too old, too rotten, and too dirty. And as time has passed they have become more and more stinking. A totally new religious consciousness is needed in the world, which will not be under any label—Hindu, Mohammedan, Christian and that is my effort. My people are not Hindu, Mohammedan, Christian, Jew ... they are just people, human beings. Naturally, every religion is against me because I am dangerous to every religion.

Strange fact: they don't agree on any point; they agree only on one point, and that is me. They agree on me, that I am wrong—about anything else they don't agree. And nobody is ready to argue with me. I have been challenging them openly, "Come face to face. And I am not calling you to my people; I will come to your congregation. And I am ready to argue with you one point by point, how you are false and how you are creating a bogus kind of religiousness"—which does not help anybody. On the contrary, it creates only wars and bloodshed.

For five thousand years how many wars they have fought, jihad, religious wars .... And they have been killing each other, and doing nothing. So my position is different from Ramakrishna Mission. And my position is also different about Ramakrishna and Vivekananda. Ramakrishna is an enlightened being, but uneducated, inarticulate—very simple, a villager. He could not create a religion; he experienced it, but he could not express it. This is one of the troubles—there are people who can express things which they have not experienced and there are people who have experienced things but they cannot express. It is not necessarily that you see the sunset and you may be able to paint it the way Picasso paints it. And it is possible Picasso may paint it without seeing it, and you have seen it but you cannot paint it—those are two different qualities. And that has created a problem.

Ramakrishna knew; Vivekananda had no experience of his own, but he became the leader of the movement. So one blind man who is articulate became the leader of other blind people. Ramakrishna is left completely out. Only his name is there; neither his experience nor his methods of experience. I have met many Ramakrishna Mission people; they don't understand Ramakrishna at all. All that they know is what Vivekananda has said. Ramakrishna never wrote a single book, never gave sermons—just sitting, talking in an ordinary way.

I strongly believe that Vivekananda was deeply influenced initially by Brahmo Samaj's preachings and then of his Guru Ramakrishna and subsequently with great philosophers like Gautama Buddha, Jesus Christ and Sankaracharaya immensely.

REFERENCES

1. Eastern and Western Disciples, Life of Swami Vivekananda, Two Volumes, Kolkata: Advaita Ashrama.

2. The Complete Works of Swami Vivekananda, Nine Volumes, Kolkata: Advaita Ashrama.

3. Romain Rolland, The Life of Vivekananda, Trans. E.K. Malcom Smith, Kolkata: Advaita Ashrama

4. Teachings of Swami Vivekananda, Kolkata: Advaita Ashrama.

Chapter 3

Swami Vivekananda The Seer As Seen By Others

Dr. R. VELMURUGAN,

Asst. Professor, Dept. of History,
K.M.Centre for P.G.Studies (Autonomous),
Lawspet, Puducherry - 605 008.

Introduction

Swami Vivekananda was the greatest sage of the 19th century who enthralled the global audience with his succinct native spiritual wisdom and exploded the wrong notions of our ancient religions and culture. When this great philosopher-saint was born on 12th January 1862, nobody would have predicted his life of immeasurable spiritual grandeur and pragmatic vision of life. He articulated the dawn of Indian Hindu Spiritual Renaissance and even beyond it. His natural intellect surpassed the dimensions of all ordinary individuals even as a child. His meeting with his guru Ramakrishna Paramahamsa[1] in Dakshineswara readily assimilated him with his master and metamorphised into leading his disciple to spread the lofty vision of our religion and culture. His quest for God was answered and the unseen Infinite was 'felt' by him.

The socio-political scenario of 19th century was highly appalling and the Indian identity and recognition were crushed by the colonial rule and thought. It was at this time, Swamiji found that our society was polluted by innumerable social evils, blind faiths and unreasonable rituals apart from stark illiteracy.[2]

The great ascetic as one chosen by God in Wordsworth's sense was not born to satisfy the paternal desire of leading a conjugal life. Saint Paramahamsa later consoled him that in the material world humans create sufferings for themselves by their narrow minds and shallow thinking. Only the spiritual thought of India could redeem the mankind from the misery. That is how his master had his first encounter with this sprawling genius of the millennium. His Guru found in him his successor and called him to lead the spiritual force into the battle to defeat the armies of evil and the forces of darkness and Narendra was rechristened as 'Swami Vivekananda'. His master laid down his mortal belongings on 15th August, 1886 to merge with the Immortal.

Swamiji stands out singularly great and impeccable in practising the life of a Yogin on one hand and complying with the real demands of the society. He did not live the life of a saffron recluse in the deep forests or in the distant Himalayas. For him, the individual liberation to understand the great 'advaitic' concept of 'Aham Brahman' and the upliftment of the society were simultaneous onerous responsibilities. He wanted to kindle the hidden spiritual power of this great country of 'tapasvis' and sustain their legacy by his articulate wisdom. He emerged as a social reformer to remove the ills and riddles of our life. Blind faith, casteism, illiteracy, untouchability, poverty and slavery were all irking realities to him. He was opposed to humans divided by caste, creed, religion, language or race.

His ebullient grace and sagacity coupled with transparent divinity elevated him to the rank and file of the world of great philosophers. His 'Chicago address' took him to the different pedestal of global recognition. The myth that was looming large among the western public that India had no religious legacy of its own was broken and the sparkling glories of our spiritual and mundane scholarship were convincingly exposed by this master.

Swamiji was one great seer of this age who spoke on all relevant aspects of humanity in general and specifically on the Indian conditions. He pleaded for women, children, youth, destitute, selfless sacrifice, eternal love for others, well-defined duties of the individuals and the like. His moral doctrines encompass the salient principles of love and compassion and his deep spiritual wisdom advocates 'advaitic' philosophy which includes according to him all the cardinal principles of monism, dualism and qualified monism. When he roared like a lion in the world conference of religions redefining the human existence in terms of eternal love and mutual universal brotherhood, he opened the gates of oriental wisdom and vision to the occidental audience. His extensive tour of Europe and America and his in-depth analysis of religions of the world and his language of love and compassion extolled the western audience. They were jolted by the ancient religious and cultural heritage and philosophy of our country. His catholic vision not confining to the portals of Hinduism as one that alone is not superior to other religions attracted the westerners towards his honesty and admission that all the religions have the same vision about life both mundane and spiritual and the ultimate goal is to understand the 'Infinite' in all of us.

Swamiji in the Eyes of Great People

Prof. Shanmugadoss of Jaffna University recalls what Swamiji spoke in Sri Lanka on his way back to India from Chicago. He pleads for tolerance of other religions. This is a matter of self-determination. The basis is understanding the divinity by oneself. The symbols must be left to the choice of the practitioner. They stand for induction. Thus Swamiji establishes the universality of all regions.[3]

It is worth recollecting what Bharathi said at this juncture.

"The joy of syntax should be like chanting of Mantras".

Those chosen mantras must congregate all the divine powers here.

Such effective vibrant 'mantras' come from Swamiji.[4] Sr. Christine adds that Swamiji often repeated what he believed. He asserted that the natural behavior of humans is essentially divine.[5]

"At one stage, he impleads that we can even set aside all Gods and Goddesses for fifty years. We have to pray only one God 'Bharatha Matha'. That was his patriotism. When someone is deeply involved intrinsically, he will become one with the object of his concentration. When 'Nammazhvar' rendered 'Nalayira Divyaprabandam' all the thoughts danced before him and vied with each other and pleaded with him to accept them." That is the intensity of his devotion. It is in consonance with Thirumular's idea. "We become the object when we assimilate ourselves with the object." Swamiji said that his energy would live with his disciples even after his mortal extinction.

Subramania Bharathi in his magazine wrote on 'Sister Nivedita'. He writes extensively on Swamiji as the very symbol of 'India's New Resurgence.'[6] Swamiji and his disciples are spreading the basic principles of Hinduism liberally like 'Pattinattar' who lost his wealth liberally. Bharathi praised him as one whose vedantic exposition itself is the basis of our nationalism.

After reading the book of Swamiji titled 'The philosophy of Yoga (Raja-Yoga)' Leo Tolstoy acknowledged the reasoning on what was man's 'self'.[7] He adds, "In Vivekananda's passionate tirades directed against the contemporary bourgeois civilization, in his affirmations of the priority of the spiritual essence of man over his 'material cover', I hear the echoes of the early teachings of the ancient Indians and particularly many motifs of the Vedas which are congenial to me". He praised Swamiji for his "excellent polemics with Schopenhauer about God".[8] Such was the magnetic impression left on the minds of one of the greatest genius of Russia.

Rabindranath Tagore admits that if anyone wants to know India, he must study the works of Swami Vivekananda. 'In him everything is positive and nothing negative.'[9] He recollects what Swamiji said that 'Narayana' (i.e., God) wanted to have our service through the poor. This is what according to Tagore is real gospel. It showed the path of infinite freedom from man's tiny egocentric self beyond the limits of all selfishness. It is not a sermon relating to a particular ritual nor is it a narrow injunction to be imposed upon one's external life. This naturally contains in it protest against untouchability not because that would make for political freedom but because that would do away with the humiliation of man, a curse which in fact puts to shame the self of us all. Is it not the greatest social responsibility that a great saint can show towards his brethren? This motto of recognizing the fellowmen and great service to humanity are universal in nature. He calls for the soul of man, not his fingers.[10] Bharathi writes in one place that the spread of Vedanta by Swamiji is the mother effort to inculcate patriotism in us.

Under the title "Ourselves", he further writes that Swamiji pumped a new spirit by his immortal address in the Chicago Conference on the principles of vedantic religion.[11] Swamiji has renounced everything in the world except his great attachment to the native soil. Even his staunch disciple Sr. Nivedita was having her reservations about it as written in 'Brabhutta Bharatham'.[12] Swamiji invoked the noble dictum that all of us should feel proud to be Indians. All Indians are our brothers. There is no distinction between the rich and the poor and discriminations in terms of caste are not relevant. We have to nourish our extraordinary courage to protect our motherland. Bharathi was astonished at Swamiji's deep scholarship, divine love and his exemplary conviction to say and do what he wanted. Even the wrongdoers and the poor in this land deserve recognition and they are also part of the ultimate divinity with which we are also in unison. This spiritual perception is universal in nature[13] and can conquer all hatred and redeem us from all the sufferings.

The detailed analysis of Swamiji's work gets more embellished when it is extrapolated by the observations of those who were equally patriotic, spiritual and scholarly. Toeing the footsteps of Bharathi, another great patriot, Subramania Siva has his own plain observations. He recalls that one of the richest women admitted that Swamiji along with German Emperor are the two greatest persons in the world. Such was his impact.[14] Former Professor of Jaffna University, Dr. Kalanithi writes that Swami Vivekananda's Vedanta treated the doctrines of all religions equal and he got the approval of the people belonging to other religions too. One can be a Hindu and still get recognised as a tolerant human being accepting the hidden treasures of other religions. Swamiji was responsible in transforming the Saivitie's mindset in Sri Lanka. Though they did not accept his Vedanta they became increasingly tolerant towards Swamiji's Vedanta.[15]

Sri Aurobindo accepts Swamiji's idea that it was in religion first that the soul of India awoke and triumphed. Once the soul of the nation was awake in religion it was only a matter of time and opportunity for it to throw itself on all spiritual and intellectual activities in the national existence and take possession of them.[16] Brahmabandhar Upadhyaya speaks that a divine light and a divine strength come from somewhere and fulfils his mind and heart in the presence of Swamiji.[17] Bal Gangadhar Tilak goes a step ahead to fix the glory of Swamiji in the Indian spiritual history. Twelve centuries ago Sankaracharaya alone spoke of the purity of our religion and its strength and wealth. It was our sacred duty according to him to take this religion in the length and breadth of the world. Vivekanada is a person of that stature who appeared towards the last half of the nineteenth century.[18]

The vision of Bipin Chandra Pal stands out significant. He believes that Swamiji is indissolubly bound up with his master, Paramahamsa Ramakrishna. Both stand almost organically bound up. The onerous burden of unfolding the mystery of Ramakrishna's vision of soul and the message of life was given to Vivekananda. Both belonged to all sects and denominations both Indian and non-Indian. Swamiji was a true universalist and the details include infinite particularities of life and thought. Vivekananda clothed this realization of his Master in the language of modern Humanism. Just as St. Paul was needed to interpret Lord Jesus, Vivekananda was necessary to explain his Master. Bipin adds that Swamiji was a nationalist and a deist to start with. His Master changed his life completely. His 'Vedanta' is exactly the message of his Master. That is why Vivekananda calls it freedom. It means removal of all outside restraint. The law of life is therefore no isolation, but association, not non-co-operation but co-operation. Freedom from the domination of our passions and appetites is the first step in the realization of the ideal. Freedom from fear and any external authority is very significant. Personal freedom through social freedom including political freedom is important to realize that one's self and God are one. This is the exact message of his Master to the modern world according to Bipin.[19] His greatest message was really the message of modern humanity. His appeal to his own people was 'Be Man.'

Nehruji called him a tonic to the depressed and demoralized Hindu mind and gave it self-reliance and some roots in the past.[20] Though Swamiji never gave any political message, everyone who came into contact with him or his writings developed a spirit of patriotism and political mentality. For Bengal, he became the father of the modern nationalist movement.[21] He died at 39 in 1902, but since his death, his influence has been even greater.[22] His concern for the poor, was very exacting. The word 'Daridranarayana' was coined by Vivekananda and popularized by Gandhiji.[23] He advised us to dedicate ourselves to the service of 'daridranarayana' and to their upliftment and edification.

The westerners were more astonished and aghast at his sharp intelligence. His charity of thought, logic of presentation and choice of diction had no parallel. Romain Rolland called him energy personified and action was his message to man. For him, as for Bethoven, it was the root of all the virtues. He was definitely a great phenomenon of 19th century. Though he died young, the flame of his pyre is still alight today. From his ashes like those of the phoenix of old, has sprung a new conscience of India. It is deep rooted from vedic times through time immemorial.

Conclusion

Thus one can gauge very easily that the very life and teachings of Swamiji had universal appeal and continue to have the same relevance and dire need even after 150 years of his birth. His global appeal in the realm of spiritualism and worldly realities are cutting across all limitations and invoking the humanity to think high and live as 'worthy men.'

REFERENCES

1. Swami Vivekananda, The heaven of the spiritual light of India, Manoj Publications, New Delhi, 2009, P.34.
2. Ibid., P.34.
3. Pe. Su. Mani (ed.) Prof. A. Shanmugadoss, Tamizhar Parvayil Swami Vivekanandar. Meyyappan Pathipagam, Chidambaram, P.94.
4. Ibid., Swami Vimurthanandar, Vivekanandarin Mandira Varthaigal, P.30.
5. Ibid., P.24.
6. 'India', November, 1906.
7. Complete Collection of Works of Tolstoy, Vol.69, P.146.
8. D.P. Makovitsky, Yasnaya Polyana Notes, Entry of 3rd July, 1908.
9. Rabindranath told this to Romain Rolland and the letter reported it to Swami Ashokananda of the Ramakrishna Mission in one of his letters.
10. Sri Aurobindo, Vol.17, 1971, P.332.
11. C. Bharathi (ed.), Bala Bharata, May, 1908.
12. Pe. Su. Mani (ed.), Op.cit., P.65.
13. Annual Member, Swadesamitran, 1920.
14. Subramanya Sivam, 'Acharya Purushar Vivekanandar' as in Pe. Su. Mani (ed.), Op.cit., P.74.
15. Pe. Su. Mani, Op.cit., P.91.
16. Sri Aurobindo, Vol.2, 1972, P.37
17. Vivekananda of Samakatin Bharatvarsa, Vol.I, Mandel Book House, Calcutta, 1982, P.351.
18. Kesari, 8th July, 1902.
19. 'Prabuddha Bharata', July, 1932, Pp.323-325.
20. J. Nehru, The Discovery of India, Meridian Books Limited, London, 1960, P.338.
21. Swami Vivekananda, My India - The India Eternal, R.K. Institute of Culture, Kolkata, 1993, P.209.
22. Prabuddha Bharata, May 1963, Pp.172-173.
23. The Indian Struggle, Asia Publishing House, Bombay, 1964, P.21.

⧼ Chapter 4 ⧽

An Exegesis of Swami Vivekananda's Poems

Dr. Lily Arul Sharmila

Asst. Prof. of English
Tagore Arts College
Puducherry-8.

The present chapter dwells upon the fundamental excellences of Swami Vivekananda's poetic art that strike the combination of things hinging on the texture of metaphysics, national character and the fruition of human existence. The smart exposition of celestial thoughts is splendid indeed as they are drawn consistently in literary studies. Swami Vivekananda's poetic work encompasses eight volumes unfathomable in their measure, magnitude, insight and versatility. Every branch of knowledge claims Vivekananda to be its own and the history of Indian writings in English too basks in the glory of accommodating unique flavour of his poetic art. It is obvious that criticism evolves down the ages on his writings. Handling Bangla and English as basic vehicles of expression, Swami Vivekananda set to work on the spiritual scruples of Sanskrit, for the texture and fabrics of his verses.

Three major poems titled, **Peace, A Quest for God** and **To the Awakened India** have been interpreted so as to scrutinize the underlying principles ranging from higher enjoyment to heritage enthusiasm, the key note and the pivot upon which his entire poetic endeavour turns. Swami Vivekananda, a *sanyasi* and a missionary has seized upon a true purpose during the hours of intuition. The objective at core is to benchmark the creation of vibrant society calling people to revamp and to play a new global role in such a highly pluralistic world.

The present chapter is an exegesis of Swami Vivekananda's poems, highlighting primarily his endless vision, perceptions and ideals on the advancement of humanity, the preservation of human harmony, order and social happiness by means of cherishing higher forms of thoughts. He expresses his incessant concern for the social degradation with apt admonition, yearning for the future want of change. He instructs man to advocate certain modes of preserving social well-being, embracing issues pertaining to the human growth, renewal of spirit and social justice. He emphasizes on the need for upbuilding moral and intellectual sustenance of the Mankind. The excellence of man was in his mind with a predominant focus on great detail to strengthen social fabrics. The indifference and callousness to complexity lend to the portion of chaos and disorientation of scruples in Indian society.

The basic tenets of evolution lie in the improvement of man through mental growth to initiate mission modes. The impediments and affectation should be cautiously cleared and the tinge of influence and inspiration must appeal to the ordinary man. These scruples embedded in the poems of Swami Vivekananda take their origin from the passion, compassion and concern for the burden hearted with lacerated feelings. His evolutionary principles are too illuminating so as to impart the mental health, constituting the relaxed, softened attitude and emotional capability for the prosperous state of the Mankind.

Swami Vivekananda (1863-1902), a celebrated poet, a visionary genius, a saint, and a mystic, who dwelt upon the actuality of human living, was entirely devoted to the cause of Mankind yet reached a dizzy height in the phenomenon of unknown. K. R. Srinivasa Iyengar praises Swami Vivekananda as a visionary genius and critiquing on his poetry he observes, "Almost an apocalyptic vision of the breaking of the worlds and the Dance of Doom..." (p.52).

The poems of Swami Vivekananda mirror the deliberate critical thinking and evolutionary thoughts on human life. They constitute a valuable body of comments and critical conjectures on the progressive aspect of human living. The fabulous feature in the multifaceted genius of the holy leader of colonial India is exemplified in his variety of poems such as **Angels Unawares, A Hymn to the Divine Mother, A Hymn to the Divinity of Shri Ramakrishna Paramahamsa, An Unfinished, An Untitled Poem on Shri Ramakrishna Paramahamsa, Blessing to Nivedita, Chorus of Cowherds, Glory unto Radha, Kali, The Mother Light, No one to Blame, On the Sea's Boson, One Circle More and The Song of Sanyaasi.**

The practical speculation expressive of his will, spirit, genius promotes not only the personal conduct of the individual but also harmonious development of the society, striking a balance between the need of the individual and the society. He has succeeded in interpreting the nation's aspiration and hope, recording her attainments of glorious past. His poems are the expressions of his visions in poetic beauty on the development of India and the formation of national character. His poems, recommend the indestructible vitality of vision in life which forms the integral part of his poetic contribution. The higher forms of achievement, culture and creative power of the masses take the nation to the dizzy heights. As an enlightened artist, he insists upon the daring need to tame and conquer the new world for the praiseworthy venture into universe. He dreamt about the formation of a well ordered society and the awakening of human mind and urged people not to be guided by the forces of disintegration.

"Strong steady blissful bold free

Awakener ever forward

Speak thy stirring words

For sleep it was not death to bring the life new..."

(To the Awakened India)

29

Peace is the poem that intensely excites and elevates the human soul by virtue of adhering to new regulations, spiritual laws and guidelines. The virtue peace recommended is the sole legitimate province of his works. Swami Vivekananda had the mental disposition to represent the sacred and intense sublimation of man's soul to contemplate upon the beautiful virtues. The subject 'peace' in his poem is the excitement, holding a door open for realizing one's dream, passion and inclination to fight against the trail of destruction. The poet makes a protracted emphasis on the essence of the fire kindling to promote the universal understanding of the Mankind for the replication of corrupt practices. Peace continues to be the most sought after. Peace is the finest element that reveals the cultural identity of one's nation, during this coordination era of today. This poem conveys a proliferation of ideals on stateliness and infuses a state of mental tranquility. The moral grandeur and spiritual health enlighten man's stand against irregularities and anomalies. The human world must vibrate blissful vibes to create more integrated global community with a sense of accountability. The poem **Peace** produces an unspeakably superior impression and the effect of morals to the readers for the harmonious interaction in human affairs. The poem provides the best source of intellectual stimulus for the readers to explore the interest to learn social, economical and intellectual holistic freedom. The essence of the poem not only enables man to extend his complete personality but also imparts him the sweetness of joy with a realization that life of man is a journey of ongoing quest for achieving supreme excellence.

"Behold it comes in might

Light that is no darkness

Shad in dazzling light..."

(To the Awakened India)

The multitude voices counselling different things, viz., a high sense, forms, profound and fertility of thoughts, opulent images, boundless illustrations are the unifying elements of his verse that distinguish the *Sanyaasi* from other poets. **Peace** is power, a light in darkness; it is joy, peace never allows grief to be felt by man. Peace grants one with immortal life. It is embodied as sweet rest in music, pause in sacred art; it is a passion, calmness of heart, unseen beauty, love that stands alone, unsung song, soothing in storms, solace that drives away the tear drops. It spreads on smiling form. Peace is the prime objective in life and the only abode in our life. The world in which, the incessant state of mental anguish prolongs and the creation of joy, the cultivation of serene mental state and intrinsic culture of accommodation and tolerance become the issues of greater import for the contemporary world to fulfil the vacuum posed by the chaotic state of affairs with jocund company of ascribed merits.

"It is joy that never spoke

grief unfelt

Immortal life unlived..."

(Peace)

The poem, **To the Awakened India** submits his poetical account of the social norms and cultural expectations which must take the central stage and enlighten men in their stand against pernicious influence. The native land put her strength in man and native land blesses him to demean the dark period as a bad joke or horrifying nightmare. Though a nation is a paragon of paradoxes, incredible ironies, a bundle of bewildering contradictions, it is a mindset of the people to seek out rationality and justice to reign supreme. People must make a paradigm shift in the developmental approaches. They must emphatically endorse their efforts to a new destiny. The diligent work has alone whetted the appetite of the people and stimulated them with credibility, conviction and innovation which are the common traits of Indian character. The Peace from the serene blessed mood offered by the objects of nature bucks up and saves Mankind as Mother Earth counts on us. A tremendous change should characterize the world and the transition that swept across India must extend to realm of civilization and culture. The critical stances of Murti attempt to read the poetry of Swami Vivekananda as representations of Indian metaphysics. He also asserts "the poetic works of Swami Vivekananda proclaim Indian culture and spiritualism of the Western readers." Swami Vivekananda ushers progress in man which would in turn transcend the adversity to opportunity. Indians wish to throw aside the burdens and it is their zest not the violence that would rule the world in future. God reveals in all as the power and life, giving untiring strength.

Swami Vivekananda's clarion call for man to move forward

Swami Vivekananda makes a clarion call for a revamp and to play a new global role. The objective at the core is to benchmark the creation of a vibrant society. Man is made to live for the pursuit of virtue and knowledge.

> "Awake, arise and dream no more
>
> Be bold and face the truth
>
> True dreams
>
> Which are eternal love, service free
>
> Truth and truth alone in all its glory shies..."

(To the Awakened India)

Swami Vivekananda has showcased in the most favourable delight that speaking stirring words to man to rise up and overcome the anguish with spirit and overting the sign of mud sputtering to probe further to reform every error by faith alone account for salvation. The blind life of man is so debased; fraud is man's peculiar vice. Swami Vivekananda puts forth determinants to save the generations from the scourge of dark period which in life time has brought the untold sorrow to mankind and reaffirmed faith for human dignity and worth. Every average Indian must be active and intelligent to rise up and overcome the anguish with spirit. Man must arm himself with a sense of fortitude with the blessedness of labour. The world should change its countenance to have a spring step.

A Vision on Starting Afresh

> "For working wonders new
>
> All things come back to the source
>
> They spring their strength to renew..."

(Peace)

Swami Vivekananda gospels on victory messages with the images of execution though a system that fails to honour the innocent and punish the wicked and guilty, the state being lashed by poverty and hunger, the public remaining exposed to terrorism, laughter that gets strained and humour to turn dark, people must work assuming positive self-image and their success is for certain rooted in their agenda. Every man must act upon new principles, entertain new ideas, forms and opinions to help harness the rational thinking in himself.

The Eyes for Vision

Our nation brings out the wealth of bliss and blithe, gay, glee and gentle peace, redefining the concept of progress situation. Our country must put a positive gloss in the lack lustre atmosphere and forward its competence profile in all compartments of life. Swami Vivekananda's verses act as an instrument of propagating the thoughts of Indian spiritual mind through English poetry. Murti says,

> "His poem, **Mother Kali,** an illuminary poetic recitation is an outcome of terrible vision on Kali - the powerful destructing agent moving around the canopy of life. It was an ecstatic trance obtained during his visit to the Bhavani temple..." (p.20.)

Swami Vivekananda has composed his poem **To the Awakened India** with a heritage enthusiasm in order to fortify the fabrics of social unit. He probes deep to identify the victory message, to initiate his mission mode and to fulfil the Divinity ordained, the honoured enterprise, as the representation of the celestial features to the world of Mankind and satisfies the innate flame of zest set ablaze in varied realms of understanding. The metaphysical treatise of Swami Vivekananda expostulates not the arid intellect of a great mind but the spontaneous springing up of the heart deeply stirred. The doctrines propagated in the poems are more pragmatic, richly laden with humanistic and religious fervour. The new atmosphere of 19th century with the synchronized rhythms of his dreams witnessed the upsurging affirmation, possible under materialistic facades. The Gita was felt to be reinterpreted without losing the original flavour of very consistent harmony. The flame set in the mind of Swami Vivekananda was fuelled by the exemplary and transcendental life of his master Ramakrishna Paramahamsa. "The seers great....the father of the race who felt the heart of truth the same and bravely taught to man ill voiced..." (To the Awakened India).

Swami Vivekananda could apprehend what the entire contour of Sastras really meant. He upholds the view that the illuminary life of the master revealed to him the import of the Vedas, the Vedanta and God, signifying the meaning of knowledge, love and sacrifice, catholicity, the objective to serve the humanity and to involve in struggles linked with wider social changes.

The impassioned cry of Swami Vivekananda aids one to draw nigh to his fellow human beings. The religious experiences communicated in his works are centred on the brotherhood of man, motherhood of deity, neighbourhood of pain, peace, self-awakening and devotion to God.

The poems of Swami Vivekananda are foregrounded in the firm tradition, metaphysics, religious principles and the ethical approaches of India. The sublime thoughts and the prophetic voices that resound all through his poems epitomize two characteristics of his personality—poetic fantasy and spiritual aspiration which are entwined in his poems. Calling our attention to this, the critic Murti exclaims at the elevated and magnificent poetic art of Swami Vivekananda,

> "His poetry is a splendid blend of immense poetic sensibility and sprinted profundity, intellectual brilliance and indefatigable energy, unselfconscious devotion, quest, innate mystic effluence, self-realization and consequent philosophic offspring—all are there converged in his poetry inseparably fused." (p.11-12)

The stages of spiritual evolution in his poems stressed upon man's ability to crush down the cascading effect of vileness. Knowledge which is nothing but action becomes a mighty tool to attack imminently on the audacious atheism, the major offshoot of evil propensities in the world. The sapient guides of spirituality who consider vileness as the product of dissention, prejudice and ugly manifestation sow the seeds of eternal verities to annex the fervour human values with the functioning of human mind.

A man who waits upon the hours of spiritual experience aspires for grasping the essence of truth. This directive is universal. According to Swami Vivekananda, the grandiose of life rests upon the practice of eternal values during earthly journey. His concept of religion borders on the virtues like purity, perseverance and the acceptance of religious truth which unveil a slew of measures to the secret of successful life through education not through the enjoyment of the corporeal pleasure.

The veracity exposes that the contemplative musing in poetic cadences imbues the feature of magnificence in Indian English poetry. Such a splendid stature has a genesis from the Divinity ordained mission of Swami Vivekananda, the forerunner of Renaissance in India. India salutes him as a messiah of service to Mankind.

REFERENCES

1. Cousin James, *The Complete Work of Swami Vivekananda*, Vol. IV, Calcutta, Advaita Ashrama, 1989.

2. Iyengar, K.R. Srinivasan, *Indian Writing in English*, New Delhi, Sterling, 1984.

3. Murthi, K., *The Poetry of Swami Vivekananda, Critical Studies in Indian Writing in English Literature*, New Delhi, Sterling, 1987, p.11-19.

4. Rolland Romain, *The Life of Universal*, Gospel S Malcom Smith Trans, Kolkatta.

5. Burke, Marie Louise, *Swami Vivekananda in America: New Discoveries*, Calcutta, Advaita Ashrama, 1958.

6. Dhar, S.N., *Swami Vivekananda*, 2 Volumes, Madras; Vivekananda Prakashan Kendra, 1975.

7. Shasidar Kumar, *Life of Swami Vivekananda by his Eastern and Western Disciples*, Calcutta: Advaita Ashrama, 1974.

8. Majumdar, R.C., (ed.) *Swami Vivekananda's Centenary Memorial Volume*, Calcutta, Swami Vivekananda Centenary Committee, 1963.

9. Rao, V.K., R.V., *Swami Vivekananda and The Universal Gospel*, Trans. E.F. Malcolm Smith, Calcutta; Advaita Ashrama, 1931.

10. M.K. Naik, *A History of Indian English Literature*, Sahitya Academy, New Delhi, 1982.

11. M.K. Naik, *Aspects of Indian Writings in English*, Macmillan, Calcutta, 1979.

Chapter 5

Impact of Swami Vivekananda on the National Movement

Dr. V. Yesubhakthan

Associate Professor
Department of Historical Studies
Ramakrishna Mission Vivekananda College
Mylapore, Chennai-600 004.

The awakening of national consciousness manifested itself in the realms of religion, philosophy, culture and society and then in the political sphere. Swami Vivekananda, whose real name was Narendranath Dutta (1863-1902), was born in an aristocratic Kasyastha family of Calcutta. His intellect was phenomenal, inspired by western science and literature. He was an anti-thesis to his master Sri Ramakrishna Paramahamsa at the beginning, later he was attracted by his master. Hinduism for Vivekananda was a universal gospel of ethical humanism and spiritual idealism. He took the spiritual world. He was hailed as the "Cyclonic Hindu" and "Hindu Napoleon". He tried to synthesis Indian spiritualism with western materialism in order to evolve a synthetic culture suited to the modern needs of a man. He urged his fellowmen to arise, awake and not to stop till they conquer the world with their spirituality. His thunderous speeches reverberated from Kanyakumari to Chicago.

When the nation was seized with apathy, inertia and despair, Swami Vivekananda's speeches and writings had contributed in strengthening the moral foundations of Indian Nationalism. He was an embodiment of emotional patriotism and a spiritual precursor of the Indian freedom movement. Thus Swami Vivekananda brought a new vigour to the dormant qualities of the people and roused the patriotic spirit of Indians. He invested the idea of service in his countrymen. Swami Vivekananda had influenced Aurobindo Ghose, Subash Chandra Bose, B.G.Tilak, Gandhiji, Nehru and several other freedom fighters. Swami Vivekananda was the patriot–prophet and spiritual nationalist of modern India.

This chapter analyses the speeches and writings of Swami Vivekananda and his influence on Indian leaders and society in strengthening fervent nationalism.

Swami Vivekananda fostered the nascent Indian Nationalism both by his life and percept. His great triumph in the Parliament of Religions at Chicago indirectly helped the cause of Indian Nationalism by raising the Indians from the slough of despair and despondency into which they had fallen and awakened them to a sense of pride in their own greatness which lies at the root of Indian Nationalism[1].

In cause of his reply to a parting address given to him by the junior Sanyasins of the Belur Math on 19 June, 1899, Swami Vivekananda said, "Remember that the aim of this institution is to make man. You must not merely learn what the Rishis taught, those Rishis are gone, their opinions are also gone with them. You must be Rishis yourselves. You are also men as much as the great men that were ever born. What can the mantras and tantras do? You must stand on your own feet. You must have this new method, the method of man-making".[2]

The ferment created by Swami Vivekananda in the intellectual plane, bursts forth after his death in Bengal and later spread everywhere as the "Revolutionary movement" led by another great man, Aurobindo Ghose.[3] Romain Rolland, the French biographer of Swami Vivekananda says "The Indian nationalist movement smouldered for a long time until Swami Vivekananda's breath blew the ashes into flame and erupted violently three years after his death in 1905". He further says, "It is an undoubted fact that the Neo Vedantism of Swami Vivekananda materially contributed this evolution".[4]

Swamiji proclaimed "If there is a sin in the world, it is weakness: avoid all weakness, weakness is sin, weakness is death. What our country now wants are muscles of iron and nerves of steel, gigantic wills which nothing can resist, which can penetrate into the mysteries and secretes of the universe, and will accomplish their purpose in any fashion , even if it meant going down to the bottom of the ocean and meeting death face to face".[5]

The basic privilege that each individual would expect in an ideal society is that of freedom or liberty to grow. Liberty is the first condition of growth. To advance oneself towards freedom—physical, mental and spiritual—and help others to do so is the supreme goal of human life of growth and well being. Where it does not exist? The man, the race, the nation must go down.[6]

Swamiji was so emphatic on the issue of liberty that he did not hesitate to proclaim non-conformity to be a virtue and sign of life. He was merely against artificial, mechanical and oppressive laws which obstruct free and unfettered growth of an individual. Consciousness would find ways and means to overcome such barriers. However, liberty according to him is not licentiousness. Liberty of one individual is bounded by the liberty of another. Man must have liberty to think and speak, in food, dress and marriage and in every sphere so long as he does not injure others.[7]

Swamijis lecture on "The future of India", states, "The problems of India are more complicated, more momentous than the problems in any other country. Race, religion, language, and government all these together make a nation. Therefore, the first plan is the making of a future India is this unification of religion. I do not mean to say that political or social improvements are not necessary but what I mean is that religion is primary".[8]

Swami Vivekananda was intensely patriotic. He says, "Oh brave one, take courage, be proud that you are an Indian" and proudly proclaim, "I am Indian, every Indian is my brother". Further he exhorts, say brother, "The soil of India is my highest heaven, India's good is my good". Thus, he was out and out 100% Indian in the dark days of Indian Patriotism.

He saw that the meeting place where all sects and castes and peoples of Hindustan could unite, would be in the spirit of an organized brotherhood, of an organized public life and in that of an organized feeling of responsibility on the part of all educated Indians to the masses[9].

The idea of nationality of Swami Vivekananda was "a sacred ideal, whose inmost striving was to express its own conception of ideal manhood".[10]

In the hard years of colonial rule, the inhuman exploitation of the Indian people and the constant attempts to trample upon their dignity and national pride, Swami Vivekananda was one of the few men in India who dared to come out boldly in defense of his people. In the struggle against colonial oppression, Swami Vivekananda sought to find support in ancient Indian traditions particularly religious ideology. He also strove to interpret religious tenets and dogmas of Hinduism in such a way to place religion at the defense of India's national interests, to unite the people to fight for independence.

Swami Vivekananda loved his motherland and its people. Herein lay the power of patriotism, the significance of his entire selfless life sacrificed on the altar of the motherland. For him India was the only sky, the welfare of India was his welfare. Swami Vivekananda said: "Remember always that there is not in the world any other country whose institutions are really better in their aims and objects than the institutions of this land".[11]

Another aspect of Swami Vivekananda's worldly outlook should be mentioned: his fervent desire to unite the people of India, his assertion that India was one state, notwithstanding the desire of the colonists to stamp out the age old striving of the people of India for consolidation. Although in this assertion, Swami Vivekananda proceeded above all from an idealistic concept of the unity of the people's spirit based on a common religion, nevertheless this does not minimize the role his views have played in creating present day India as a united, monolithic and peace loving state.

Swami Vivekananda's impassioned call to general fraternity and unity of India's people, to the abolition of religious and communal discard and of caste prejudices were combined with an appeal for peace and friendship among all the nations of the world, which is the cornerstone of Indian tradition, the main content of the Indian national character.

Swami Vivekananda persistently sought a way out of his country's plight. Although his socio-economic and political views had elements of eclecticism, a combination of spontaneous rebellious spirit against social injustice, social utopia of the ideas of reformism and revolutionary protest, notwithstanding the historical conditioning and class limitations of his philosophical and sociological views, his worldly outlook as a whole played a constructive part in the development of national liberation movement in India, in rallying the Indian people to struggle against colonialism.[12]

The elements which compose the nations of the world are indeed very few, taking race, after race, compared to this country. They were the Aryan, the Dravidian, the Tartar, the Turk, the Mughal, and the European, all the nations of the world as it were, pouring their blood into this land. Of languages, the most wonderful conglomeration is here of manners and customs, there is more difference between two Indian races than between the European and Eastern races.

The one common ground that we have is our sacred tradition, our religion. That is the only common ground, and upon that we shall have to build. In Europe political ideas form the national unity. In Asia, religious ideals form the national unity. The unity in religion therefore, is absolutely necessary as the first condition of the future of India.[13]

We see how in Asia and especially in India, race difficulties, linguistic difficulties, social difficulties, national difficulties, all met away before this unifying power of religion. We know that to the Indian mind there is nothing higher than religious ideals that is the key note of Indian life, and we can only work in the line of least resistance. It is not only true that the ideal of religion is the highest ideal; in the case of India it is the only possible means of work: work in any other line, without first strengthening this, would be disastrous.

We know that our religion has certain common grounds, common to all our sects, however varying their claims may be. So there are certain common grounds and within their limitations, this religion of ours admits of a marvellous variation, an infinite amount of liberty to think and live our own lives. We all know that, at least those of us who have thought: and what we want is to bring out these life giving long principles of our religion and let every man, woman and child throughout the length and breadth of this country understand them, know them and try to bring them out in their lives. This is the first step and therefore it has to be taken.[14] Let us preach where we all agree and leave the differences to remedy themselves. As I have said to the Indian people again and again, if there is the darkness of centuries in a room and we go into the room and begin to cry, oh, it is dark, it is dark! Will the darkness go? Bring the light and darkness will vanish at once.[15]

Swami Vivekananda applies traditional tenet to the ideal of international co-operation and harmony drawing conclusions which Ramakrishna would perhaps have accepted, but never himself taught or even imagined. It is the idea of the "Solidarity of the Universe", Swami Vivekananda says, "Which the world is waiting to receive from Upanishads."

Even in politics and sociology, problems that were only national twenty years ago can no more be solved on national grounds only. They are assuming huge proportions and gigantic shapes. They can only be solved when looked at in the broader light of international grounds. International organization, international combinations are the cry of the day. That is the solidarity.[16]

The aspects of Swami Vivekananda's thought which he saw not as contradictory but complementary: his claim for the uniqueness of Indian wisdom, which strengthened his appeal to the Indian nationalists, is combined with a forceful advocacy of international solidarity. Once again, this may be seen in the light of his ideas on evolution: the harmony of mankind is the highest stage, and logical consequence, of an increasing self realization by individuals within society: only ignorance inhibits man's natural growth towards freedom and harmony. The fact that Swami Vivekananda's thought inspired forms of extreme Indian Nationalism is understandable, but nationalism, for Swami Vivekananda is an incomplete stage of development. "There is but one basis of well being" he said "social, political or spiritual to know that I and my brother are one. This is true for all countries and all people"[17].

The idea of freedom emerged in nineteenth century India; it dominated the political thought of the twentieth century. In one sense, this appears only natural, for India during much of this time was engaged in a serious struggle for independence; and for many of the Indian nationalists freedom meant no more than termination of foreign rule. Among India's leading thinkers, however, a philosophy of freedom was developed, that affirmed, on the one hand, the goal of political independence, but insisted on the other, that independence, of itself, was incomplete: that it must be fulfilled through a realization by each individual of moral and spiritual freedom. In this way, they believed, freedom would assume new meaning in the discovery of a natural correspondence with equality and harmony. Their attempts must be seen as part of a response to the western political and social ideals of liberty and equality: these values were thought desirable but not, in themselves, sufficient. The task which Swami Vivekananda inspired and later Indian thinkers pursued became above all, one of completion: the bringing of fruition of both traditional Indian and modern western values by using one ethic to complement the other. In the end, the result was envisioned as a harmony of political, social and spiritual ideals.[18]

Conclusion

Swami Vivekananda was an ardent patriot, with an immense love for the country and its culture. He played the most significant role of any nineteenth century Indian thinker. His search for a melody among the discordant notes of his century was representative rather than unique. His singular achievement rests with the thematic rhythm he introduced, which resounded the ideas of Aurobindo Ghose, Tagore Gandhiji, Subash Chandra Bose and other freedom fighters.

REFERENCES

1. Swami Vivekananda centenary memorial volume, (Ed) R.C.Majumdar, Calcutta-1963.P.499.

2. Complete works of Swami Vivekananda, Vol.V, 3rd Edition P.152

3. Datta Bhupendranath, Swami Vivekananda, patriot-prophet-A study, Calcutta, 1954, P.213.

4. Ibid.

5. Swami Vivekananda centenary memorial, Op.cit., P.499

6. Arun Kumar Biswas, Swami Vivekananda centenary memorial volume, (Ed) R.C. Majumdar, Calcutta-1963.P.495 and the Indian quest for socialism Firmaklm Pvt. Ltd., Calcutta, 1986.P.74

7. Ibid P.75

8. Bhupendranath Datta, Op-Cit PP.318-319

9. Ibid, 324

10. Ibid, 326

11. Swami Vivekananda centenary memorial volume, Op.cit P.513

12. Ibid, P.517

13. Swami Vivekananda, My India, The India Eternal, Ramakrishna Mission Institute of culture, Calcutta, 1996.P.116

14. Ibid, P118

15. Ibid

16. Dennis Dalton, Political thought of Swami Vivekananda centenary memorial volume, (Ed) R.C.Majumdar, Calcutta-1963.P.495, Aurobindo Ghose, Rabindranth Tagore and Mahatma Gandhi, The academic press, Gurgaon, 1982.P.82

17. Ibid, P.83

18. Ibid, P.84

∽ Chapter 6 ∼

The Social Service of Swami Vivekananda and Sri Narayanaguru: A Comparative Study

Dr. Manickam

Associate Professor of History
Avvaiyar Govt College for Women Karaikal,
U.T of Puducherry

Indian society underwent an immense and radical change due to a variety of factors by the middle of the 19th century. Several influences of social, communal and religious reforming activities arose all over India. These social and religious reform movements such as Brahma Samaj, Arya Samaj, Theosophical society, S.N.D.P movement, Ramakrishna Mission, Self Respect Movement, etc., were continuously established with serious and noble cause one after another by several social leaders to purify the Hindu religion and society.

The leaders of the aforesaid movements had been persistently and constantly functioning with a view to elevate the depressed category of Hindu society in divergent parts of India. Their social services had greater significance in the beginning of the twentieth century.

The present chapter attempts to delineate the dexterous and remarkable social services Swami Vivekananda and Sri Narayanaguru rendered to the Hindu society.

In fact, during the middle of the 19th century, the Indian society consisted of four Varnas namely the Brahmina, the Kshatriya, the Vaishya and the Sudra, and a large number of caste and sub caste system and multi-religious and racial groups. It is by and large believed that after the arrival of the Aryans in India, the varna (colour) and caste system was deep-rooted in the Indian soil particularly in the Hindu society and religion[1]. Hence, the varna and caste system had been vulnerably prevalent among the Hindus, who were segregated into a large and divergent number of castes and sub castes. Both varna and caste system coexisted with one another and these were an integral part of Hindu society.

According to both varna and caste hierarchy, the Brahmins invariably occupied the uppermost position in the Hindu social order. Right from the beginning, they were considered as a great divinity in the form of human being and were given numerous and abundant privileges and constitutional rights in the society.

They dominated the Hindu society not because of their higher social strata but primarily because of their foremost position in economic and educational spheres. They portrayed themselves as supreme priests, scholars and philosophers due to their mastery over and fluency in Sanskrit language and their sophistication in performing rituals[2]. They enjoyed incredible, remarkable and undue reverence even at the court of local rulers. They had easy, trouble-free and more access to higher education and white collar jobs in the government under British rule than other caste people. They exploited the prejudiced caste system and religion as their foremost and core weapons to overpower the downtrodden people in countless ways in the Hindu society.

The miserable class people were continuously persecuted by the caste Hindus particularly, the Brahmins. For instance, the right of admission to public schools, direct recruitment to govt. services, entry into public roads and temples of caste Hindus, learning Sanskrit language, listening to vedas and other sacred scriptures, taking drinking water and using public wells and tanks, dressing in Hindu style, wearing certain ornaments and sandals, using umbrella in some regions and political representations were forbidden by the caste Hindus for dismayed and distressed people, who suffered from many civic and religious disabilities[3].

Apart from these, there were some practices such as child marriage, prohibition of widow remarriage, Sati, polygamy, inequality, injustice, untouchability, purdha system, prostitution and devadasi system in the Hindu society[4]. The economically depressed people were pushed down below the line of poverty and were humiliated by the caste Hindus in diverse ways. Thus, they were kept away from the caste Hindus' residences and were prevented from taking part in important rituals.

Under these circumstances, the introduction of western system of education by British Government, opening of schools and colleges, orphanages and providing free food and clothes for non-Brahmins by the Christian missionaries not only opened the eyes of the depressed class people but also awakened them to fight against their ill treatment and insults constantly unleashed by the caste Hindus in the society[5].

Comparatively speaking Swami Vivekananda and Sri Narayanaguru were two vibrant, vivacious and spiritual saints. They were great reformers and philosophers at the dawn of the 20th century in India. In many a sense their services have ethical, political, spiritual and social dimensions.

Swami Vivekananda was born in 1863 in a Brahmin family in West Bengal. But Sri Narayanaguru was born in 1855 in Izhava community in Kerala state. Swami Vivekananda after having graduation from Calcutta University, learned ancient Hindu Philosophy from Sri Ramakrishna Paramahamsa whereas Sri Narayanaguru received his education in Sanskrit, Malayalam, Tamil and Astrology from his father Madan Asan, a poor school teacher and learned Vedas, Vedanta and Advaita of Adi Shankaracharya from Kummampalli Raman Pillai, an eminent scholar[6].

When Hinduism was in its decay, Swami Vivekananda appeared as a great socio-religious reformer on the social scenery to renovate Hinduism by eradicating the custom bound and ritual ridden regressive practices of Hinduism. But in Kerala in 1890, Sri Narayanaguru emerged as a shining star to shake the foundation of wrong notions of Hinduism.

On seeing the social condition of Hindu society, Swami Vivekananda realised that Hindu social customs were not on the basis of true religious teachings of Hinduism as it had a lot of abuses and evil practices. So he felt that reformation of Hinduism was necessary for the uplift of the downtrodden masses[7]. Similar was the case with Sri Narayanaguru.

Swami Vivekananda desired to reform the Hindu society on the model of American society which he admired so much after attending the Parliament of Religions held at Chicago in 1893 and after seeing and traveling around the western world[8]. But Sri Narayanaguru wanted to reform the Hindu society by removing superstitions and meaningless practices such as giving too much importance to idol worship and similar such evils[9].

Swami Vivekananda undertook his travel all over India, suffered lot of hardships and faced hunger, cold and unfriendly weather, disease and many other challenges with resilience and courage. He delivered eloquent lectures extensively on the universal values to awaken the slumbering minds of young Indians and created spiritual and social awareness among them[10]. Likewise Sri Narayanaguru undertook arduous travels to every nook and corner of Kerala state and explained the philosophy of Hinduism in a simple manner. He also preached his revolutionary ideals of Hindu religion to the downtrodden masses[11].

Swami Vivekananda made inspiring speeches to the caste critic Indians to eradicate the humiliating caste system from Hindu society. He used to say, there is no caste at all but there is one caste that is humanity. He dexterously fought against the class system, inhumanism and social degradation by way of advising the Indians that the Brahmins should not be pulled down from their high position but they should raise up the rest of the society[12]. But Sri Narayanaguru condemned the Hindu caste system and vigorously made direct attack on the supremacy of the Brahmins[13].

Swami Vivekananda condemned the current practices of ritual ceremonies and superstitions and pressed the Indians to have spirit of liberty, social equality, individual freedom, justice and free thinking like western humanism and to render their social services to the depressed class people[14]. Similarly Sri Narayanaguru was also deadly against the ritual ceremonies and blind beliefs of Hinduism[15].

Swami Vivekananda realised the importance of Indian women and desired to emancipate them from their bondage. He used to say if you educate a man only one person will be educated but if you educate one woman the whole family will be educated. So he reiterated the significance of centralizing the women for better life. As a result he openly supported widow remarriage and advised the Indians to liberate and educate their women like western lines[16]. Similarly Sri Narayanaguru felt the significance of women in the Hindu society. He gave equal religious rights to them and established separate mutts for them to give religious training at Parur[17].

Swami Vivekananda condemned the wrong notion and convention of Hinduism. But Sri Narayanaguru broke the wrong convention and concept of Hinduism that only the Brahmins can recite the holy scriptures with purity by making a boy of low caste recite vedas in Sanskrit fluently among the Brahmin Pandits[18].

Swami Vivekananda worked for universal concept. While giving a new theory of ethics and new principles of morality he advocated that we should love and serve our neighbours because we are all one before the supreme spirit known as Paramatma[19]. But Sri Narayanaguru followed monotheism and challenged all the wrong ideals, philosophy, doctrines and beliefs of Hinduism. He believed that man himself was God and by serving mankind one could realise God. He constructed many temples and shrines all over Kerala and placed mirror and plaques instead of keeping idols in some temples. He invited people without race and religion to worship God in the temples. He made them to realise the supreme truth that God is one and all are equal before Him[20].

In 1894, Swami Vivekananda founded Ramakrishna Mission for propagating education like western lines along with spirituality among the masses[21]. This mission stood for monastic order and to reform the Hindu society without violation. Similarly Sri Narayanaguru established Sri Narayana Dharma Paripalana Sangam in January 1928 to carry on his teachings, religious and social works in Kerala state[22].

The Ramakrishna Mission opened a number of schools and colleges all over India for imparting education along with spirituality to young Indians[23]. Likewise Sri Narayanaguru established several educational institutions in different parts of Kerala state to educate Vedas and Vedantas to the students of low caste[24].

The Ramakrishna Mission undertook the propagation of practical Vedanta and various types of social works such as running hospitals, dispensaries, hostels, libraries, orphanages, rural development centres, etc. Swami Vivekananda also conducted massive reliefs and rehabilitation work for the victims of the natural calamities such as earthquake, cyclones in different parts of India and other countries[25]. This mission followed the idea of pivotal elimination of any distasting social, religious, racial and communal practices.

The Mission was open to all men without any distinction of religion, race and caste. Many western people were influenced by the life and message of Swami Vivekananda and some of them became his friends and disciples. Among them, a very important person was Margaret Nolado, known as sister Nivetha[26].

Referring to his religious and social services to the Indians, Pandit Jawaharlal Nehru, the first Prime Minister of India praised him that "he (Vivekananda) came as a tonic to the depressed and demoralized Hindu mind and gave it self reliance and some roots in the past.[27]"

Sri Narayanaguru established several mutts and ashrams in different parts of Kerala. He admitted the students of Izhavas, Cherumas, Pulaya and Paraiah castes without any caste discrimination in his mutts and ashrams and taught them moral values, Vedas and Vedanta in Sanskrit[28]. He advised them to work for the abolition of caste system.

These mutts gave equal education and religious teaching to many non-brahmin students to acquire high ritual status equal to that of Brahmin saints. Besides these mutts made the students to propagate the religious teachings of Sri Narayanaguru to common people and gave equal status for underprivileged community[29].

The sweeping reforms and relentless struggles of these two spiritual leaders brought dignity and decency to the masses who were marginalized by the dominant community for a long period of time. Both of them perceived social service through religion.

REFERENCES

1. R.K. Kshirsadar, Dalit Movement in India and its Leader, 1857-1956, New Delhi. p31.

2. P. Subramanian, Social History of the Tamils. New Delhi, 1990 p60.

3. M.S.A. Rao, Social movement and Social Transformation. A study of two backward classes movements in India, Delhi, 1979 p

4. Ibid

5. P. Subramanian, op. cite, p 337-347

6. R.C. Majumdar, H.C. Ray Chaudhuri and K. Datta, An Advanced History of India, Madras reprint 1978.

7. P. Subramanian, Op. cite, P. 34

8. Ibid

9. M.S.A Rao, op. cite, p36.

10. P. Subramanian, op. cite, pp 281 282.

11. M.S.A Rao op. cite, p39.

12. P. Subramanian op. cite, p282.

13. M.S.A. Rao op. cite, P. 36

14. http://www.belurmath.org/swami vivekananda htm.

15. M.S.A. Rao op. cite, p40

16. P. Subramanian, Op. cite P. 282

17. M.S.A. Rao, op. cite P. 40

18. Ibid p. 37

19. http://www.belurmath.org/Swami vivekananda htm

20. M.S.A. Rao op. cite p39.

21. P. Subramanian, op. cite P. 282

22. M.S.A. Rao op. cite p42.

23. R.C. Majumdar and others. Op. cite, p875.

24. M.S.A. Rao opcite p. 39
25. R.C. Majumdar and others, page 874 and 875.
26. http:// www.belurmath.org/swami vivekananda htm
27. Ibid
28. M.S.A. Rao op. cite, 36, 37
29. Ibid. p43

✺ Chapter 7 ✺

Activities of Ramakrishna Mission in Kerala

Dr. Joy Varkey

Associate Professor of History
N.A.M. College, Kallikkandy,
Kannur, Kerala

In a meeting of the disciples of Bhagvan Sri Ramakrishna in 1898, Brahmachari Shuddhananda asked Swami Vivekananda: What would be the role of Ramakrishana Mission in the regeneration of India? Swami replied: "from this *mutt* (monastery) hundreds of men of character will go out, who will deluge the country with spirituality. This will be followed by social, political and other revitalizations. Consequently, there will come about a great transformation in Indian society".[1] Thus spiritual awakening and consequent secular regeneration, according to Vivekananda, constitute the foremost objective of Ramakrishna Mission throughout the country.

Before his *mahasamadhi*, Sri Ramakrishna had formed a *Sangha* of his disciples (order of monks) with Vivekananda, his beloved disciple, as its leader.[2] The purpose of this *Sangha* was to immerse in spirituality, i.e., the spirit of the unity of men and God. This is an inward search for Reality or Truth, which is nothing less than love of God in all men; for God is incarnate in man. At the same time, what Swami Vivekananda had done was to make an outward program of social, educational and, above all, humanitarian activities with the cooperation of laymen to reproduce the inward spiritual search initiated by Sri Ramakrishna.[3] These two indispensably complementary aspects, the inward search and outward program, represented the Ramakrishna Mutt and Ramakrishna Mission respectively. The purpose of this chapter is to discuss the activities of Ramakrishna Mission in Kerala[4] in a historical perspective with emphasis on various social and intellectual programs undertaken by the mission in different parts of the state.

Referring to his plan Swami Vivekananda said: "I want to start two institutions; one in Madras and one in Calcutta to carry out my plan; and that plan briefly is to bring the Vedantic ideals into the every-day practical life of the saint or the sinner, of sage or the ignoramus, of the Brahmin or the Pariah."[5] Hence Swami Ramakrishnananda was deputed for the propagation of the message of Ramakrishna Paramahamsa in South India. He arrived in Madras in 1897 and later on visited Bengaluru, Mysore, Trivandrum and Cochin for the propagation of the ideas and principles of his Guru Sri Ramakrishna. In 1907, an *ashram* was set up in Madras under his supervision as the headquarters of the activities of the Ramakrishna Mission in south India. Subsequently, another *ashram* was established in Bengaluru in 1909, which was placed under the supervision of Swami Nirmalananda, who played a pivotal role in the establishment of Ramakrishna *ashrams* and its mission activities in different parts of Kerala.

Establishment of Ramakrishna Ashrams in Kerala

The first Ramakrishna *ashram* or *mutt* in Kerala was established at Haripad. It was Swami Nirmalananda who laid the foundation stone for the *mutt* on 11 September 1912 and inaugurated it on 4 May 1913.[6] The land for the *ashram* was donated by one Venkata Krishna Iyyer, who later became a *sannyasi* of Ramakrishna monastic order. From its inception onwards the *ashram* gave emphasis on social service to uplift the lower caste and outcaste people. On the occasion of Ramakrishna Jayanthi in 1914 an outcaste boy was admitted as *brahmachari* in the *mutt*. The *ashram* witnessed the initiation of eleven disciples as *sannyasins* in the monastic order of Ramakrishna in 1923.[7] Thus the first *ashram* made an excellent starting of the social and religious programs of the mission. The second Ramakrishna *mutt* in Kerala was inaugurated at Thiruvalla on 9 May 1913 by Swami Nirmalananda himself. Nevertheless, as early as 1910, Sri Ramakrishna *Sangha* had been functioning in the town that took initiatives for the establishment of this *ashram*.[8]

The construction of an *ashram* at Nettayam in Trivandrum was started in 1916 with the foundation stone laid by Swami Nirmalananda, but it was inaugurated only on 7 March 1924. A plot of five acres of land was donated by a generous person Arunachalam Pillai for the *ashram*. This *ashram* is called Sri Ramakrishna Brahmananda Ashram. Besides, propagating the spiritual message of Ramakrishna and Vivekananda, this centre gave emphasis on health care services.

The Ramakrishna *Mutt* of Trichur is located at Puranattukara. The relief camp set up during the time of floods in 1924 eventually became a branch of Ramakrishna Mission with the *ashram* founded on 3 May 1927. The founder of this *ashram* was Swami Thyagisananda (his pre-*sannyasa* name V.K. Krishna Iyyer), who was lawyer-turned-teacher before taking the spiritual vocation. He had been associated with Vivekodayam Samajam in Trichur as its principal organizer, which started functioning in 1917. This *mutt* has given special attention to social, religious and educational progress of Harijans in the nearby colony. It is remarkable that Ramakrishna shrine in this Harijan colony has Harijan poojaris to perform *pooja* rituals. It is a tradition breaking practice of *pooja* that brought the outcaste to the level of upper caste, a revolutionary religious and social event aimed at establishing social equality and justice as envisaged by Swami Vivekananda.

Sri Ramakrishna Advaita Ashram in Kalady was established under the initiatives of Swami Agamananda on 26 April 1936. Like other *ashrams* this one focuses its works on social issues, education, etc. The backward colony at Mattoor near Kalady has about 500 members, all very poor and badly in need of help. The *ashram* from its own resources built some low-cost dwellings in the early seventies and gifted those houses to the neediest amongst them. Education was also a major field of service for the *ashram*.

In the Malabar region, which was under British rule before 1947, the first *ashram* was opened at Quilandy on 30 March 1915 by Swami Nirmalananda. Local people like K.P. Krishnan Nair, Kelappan Kidavu, and Ittirappa Menon worked for the establishment and functioning of the *mutt*. Activities of Ramakrishna Mission Sevashram at Calicut in the beginning were a part of the programs of the *mutt* at Quilandy. However, as early as 1913 there was a Ramakrishna Vedanta Sangha functioning at Calicut to disseminate the ideas of Ramakrishna and Vivekananda. In 1928, Swami Nirmalananda had been invited to visit Calicut and address the members of this *Sangha*. In 1937, Swamiji visited twice the Vedanta Sangha and realizing the dedication of its members, he proposed the establishment of an *ashram* in Calicut. This *ashram* came into existence in 1941 under the spiritual guidance of Swami Nirvikarananda.

Other Ramakrishna *ashrams* were founded at Alappuzha (1923), Ottapalam and Vallikkode (1926), Kayamkulam (1927), Palai and Kulathoormuzhi (1930), Muvattupuzha (1931), Adoor (1932), Puthukkad (1934), Vyttila (1947), Mattakkara (1969), Kaloor (1982), Vaikom (1994), Cherusseri (1998), Cheroor (2002), and Palemad (2010). Besides these *ashrams*, Sri Ramakrishna-Vivekananda Charitable Trust at Purameri was opened in 1991, Vivekananda Kendra Vedic Vision Foundation at Kodungallur was inaugurated in 1997, and a number of study centres at different places, etc., were opened; all these centres functioned with the single goal of spreading the message and activities of Ramakrishna Mission in Kerala.[9]

Activities of Sri Ramakrishna Mission

While the *ashram* is the residence of the *sannyasins* and centre of the spiritual training and formation for brahmacharins, the mission, normally based in the *ashram*, is the hub of social and educational services. Activities of the mission are generally concentrated in the field of anti-caste programs, Harijan services, education, medical care, and publications. However, it also appears that many *ashrams* have preferences in the matter of undertaking various services. Nowadays Sri Ramakrishna *ashram* at Purnattukara in Trichur, Sri Ramakrishna Advaita *Ashram* at Kalady, Sri Ramakrishna Mission Sevashram at Calicut and Sri Ramakrishna Brahmananda *Ashram* at Trivandrum function as prominent centres of Ramakrishna Mission in Kerala.

a) Against the Caste System

The caste system and its rules and discriminations remained awfully rude in Kerala, which were observed by Swami Vivekananda himself during his visit to various parts of this state. Subsequently, he made a stringent criticism of caste discriminations:

> Was there a sillier thing before in the world than what I saw in Malabar country? The poor Pariah is not allowed to pass through the same street as the high caste man, but if he changes his name to a hodge-podge English name, it is all right; or to a Mohammedan name, it is all right. What inference would you draw except that these Malabaris are all lunatics, their homes so many lunatic asylums, and that they are to be treated with derision by every race in India until they mend their manners and know better.[10]

It is discernible that the observation and criticism made by Swami Vivekananda indicated the utmost necessity of spiritual and secular efforts to fight against caste evils in Kerala. Further, he pointed out the significance of freedom and equality of men: "No man and no nation can attempt to gain physical freedom without physical equality, nor mental freedom without mental equality."[11] Therefore, Swami Vivekananda declared: "we do stand in need of social reform."[12]

Following the message of Vivekananda, social reform programs constituted a major field work for the Ramakrishna Mission in Kerala. Social reform movement in Kerala was largely a fight against evils of caste system, against "don't touchism" to borrow the term from Swami Vivekananda. Swami visited Kerala in 1892 following his sojourn in the Kingdom of Mysore. It appears that Swami was a guest of Dr. P. Palpu, a Keralite belonging to Ezhava caste, who was the Municipal Medical officer of Bangalore.[13] He did not get a job in his native State of Travancore because of his lower caste status. Dr. Palpu informed Swami Vivekananda "about the tyranny of higher castes over the lower caste people in his native State" in advance of his tour to Kerala.[14] Swami Vivekananda arrived in Shornur by train, then travelled to Trichur by a bullock-cart and stayed overnight in the house of D.A.Subramanya Iyyer, an officer of Education Department of Cochin State. Then he went to Ernakulam via Cranganore. He met Chattambi Swamigal at Ernakulam. His next destination was Trivandrum, where he stayed for nine days from 13 December.[15] During his travel in Kerala, Swami understood how worse was the social condition of Kerala due to "don't touchism" created by caste barricades. Therefore, Swami asserted that physical and mental freedom from the evils of caste system was indispensable to the regeneration of our society.

Right from the beginning of Ramakrishna Mission in Kerala, with the establishment of the *ashram* at Haripad, various programs for the removal of caste discriminations and attainment of freedom and equality constituted a significant field of its social work. During the first anniversary celebrations of the Haripad *mutt* in 1914, a *misra-bhojanam* (inter-caste dining), the first of its kind in Kerala, was organized as part of its fight against caste intolerance. However, after the feast, people belonging to *savarna* caste were reluctant to take the plantain leaves used by the *avarna* people. Nirmalananda Swami, who was also present in the function and noticed the *savarna* people's reluctance in cleaning the place, came himself forward to take the leaves and clean the floor.[16] It was an exemplary act of protest against caste prejudice and discriminations that persuaded the people assembled there to follow the act of Swami. It was a glorious method of man-making envisaged by Swami Vivekananda for the modernization of Indian society. Following the Haripad *misra-bhojanam*, other *ashrams* also organized such method of fight against evils of caste practices. It later on became a method of social resistance adopted by organizations of social reformers.

It is remarkable that in 1915 on the occasion of Ramakrishna Jayanthi celebrations organized by the *ashram* at Haripad, Swami

Chitsukhananda (Venkata Krishna Iyyer) arranged a procession, which was to start from the premises of Subramanya temple of Hari-pad with the participation of both high caste and outcaste people.[17] It was a procession to spread the message of the equality of all people irrespective of caste differences; an event to bring the *avarna* to the public space, especially in the precincts of a temple, which was for-bidden to them by caste rules. As mentioned earlier, the admission of an outcaste boy as brahmachari in the *ashram* in 1914 was a remarka-ble act towards the beginning of giving equal opportunity disregard-ing caste difference. Swami Vivekananda said: "the Brahmin and the Sudra and the Pariah must have equal opportunities of knowing the great truths of the Vendanta."[18]

Ramakrishna *ashrams* in many places became centres of wor-ship for the *avarna* people. The birthday celebrations of Swami Vivekananda gave an opportunity to bring lower caste and outcaste people together with the upper caste in public space. In fact, such a celebration held in Palai in 1925 attracted the *avarna* masses into Sri Ramakrishna Mission and it helped the establishment of an *ashram* there in a plot of land donated by Kunjan Chettiar in 1926.

b) Educational Services

Ramakrishna Mission gives much emphasis on the education of peo-ple, especially of the lower castes and the Harijans. During an inter-view, Swami Vivekananda was asked: "What will you propose for the improvement of your masses?" Then he said: "We have to give them secular education. We have to follow the plan laid down by our an-cestors—that is to bring down all the ideals slowly among the masses. Raise them slowly up, raise them to equality. Impart even secular knowledge through religion."[19] On another occasion, he wrote to Swami Shuddhananda "our work should be mainly educational, both moral and intellectual." [20] It "must be devoted to character-building and man-making."[21] Thus it is important to "educate our people so that they may be able to solve their own problems."[22]

The entire group of Sri Ramakrishna *ashrams* in Kerala work for the educational progress of all sections of people, especially of the depressed masses. Nevertheless, among them certain *ashrams* like Sri Ramakrishna *Ashram* in Puranattukara possesses a unique place in the field of educational services. The 1936 report of the *ashram* shows that being a rural centre situated in Puranattukara, its educational work was directed chiefly to the uplift of the downtrodden people, especially the Harijans. The upper primary school at that time had 300 pupils, of them more than half were Harijan children. The *ashram* also had Gurukula or hostel having about 30 inmates; three-fourths of whom were Harijans.[23] Besides giving religious instruction and secular education including teaching three languages—Sanskrit, Hindi and Malayalam—special care was given to develop aptitude and skill for manual work in the students. It was reported that the aim of the management was to make the school for Harijans what the Tuskegee Institute was for the African-Americans in the USA.[24] On 16 January 1934, Gandhiji had laid the foundation stone for the hostel building and temple and he stayed in the *ashram* campus in a residence named 'Anandakudirum'.

The report of the *ashram* for the year 1946 says that it was developed into an ideal centre for rural reconstruction with various departments like the high school (sanctioned in 1940) called Vidyamandir with primary and lower secondary sections, industrial school, hostel for boys called Gurukul, hostel for girls called Matrimandiram, library, co-operative society, etc. The high school had 684 students on its rolls at the end of the year. Out of the 27 students who appeared for the public examination, S.S.L.C, 13 came out successful, which was a great achievement as far as a school for Harijans was considered. The industrial school had a total strength of 46 students in 1946. Weaving, spinning, etc., were taught in the school. There were 23 looms and 25 charkas in good working condition in the school. The trained students received wages ranging from five to twenty-five rupees per month. There was a total production of cloth which was worth about Rs. 26,000/- in 1946 and expenditure by way of wages given to students was Rs. 6078/-.[25] Thus this industrial school helped students to acquire training in any trade and thereby receive some financial support in wages, while it facilitated the *ashram* to generate some revenue for its services. It is noteworthy that the Adat Harijan colony near the *ashram* has always been given special attention by the mission for the educational and social progress of Harijan children, particularly for their spiritual enlightenment.

At present the school has been upgraded to a higher second-ary school for boys, which has 1679 students and primary school has about 500 boys. There are 137 boys in the hostel; of them 16 are Harijans and 26 are orphans from various communities. The child welfare or *sisu vihar* has 25 Harijan children. The education, accom-modation and other services for the girls are now under the care of Sarada Devi Mutt. Vivekananda Vignanabhavanam which consisted of a library, reading room, Sanskrit study centre, etc., is located at Poonkunnam in Trichur town. This library has a collection of 7000 books and 18 periodicals. This centre also offers free Sanskrit classes and weekly religious classes. By the way, the libraries attached to the schools have a collection of 13,700 books.

It is also noteworthy that the Trichur Centre of the mission or-ganized rural and industrial exhibition, as part of educational and rural reconstruction program. Referring to the first exhibition held in 1939, Swami Ajarananda, Secretary of Exhibition wrote: "our pri-mary object in organizing an exhibition of this nature was to give rural population a comprehensive idea of the need and possibilities of improving agriculture, cattle-breeding and the various cottage in-dustries in our State." [26]

The Ramakrishna Mission Sevashram at Calicut also focuses its activities on education. While undertaking relief measures dur-ing the time of cholera in the 1940s, the *ashram* started an orphanage in 1944 as there came six children, the number increased to 30 or-phans by the year 1945. In the same year, the *ashram* bought a lower primary school for the education of these children, where one Hari-jan named Narayanan, who passed Teacher Training Course (T.T.C.) was appointed the headmaster. In 1952, the school was upgraded to upper primary school and in the next year it became a high school. In 1958, the new high school building was inaugurated by the then Chief Minister E.M.S. Namboothiripad. The famous children's poet Kunjunni Master was a teacher in this school at Meenchanda, in Cali-cut. At present this has been upgraded to a mixed higher secondary school, which has more than 3000 students including high school section. The primary school has about 700 students.

Sri Ramakrishna Advaita *Ashram* in Kalady is another impor-tant centre of Ramakrishna Mission in Kerala in the field of educational services. It has schools up to higher secondary level, hostel for tribal and Harijan students, typewriter and computer training centre, crèche, etc. In 1937, the *ashram* started a Sanskrit school that eventually developed as high school. The tribal hostel for boys was started in 1964 with a building grant from Government of India. According to the report for 2005-06 period, the hostel has more than 134 boys from scheduled caste and tribes and 28 paying members from forward communities. In 2005, the type writing centre had 43 trainees. The crèche had 30 kids of Harijan parents who go for work.

c) Health Care

Health care is another area of Ramakrishna Mission's activities in Kerala. Most of the *ashrams* started ayurvedic or allopathic dispensaries to provide basic medical care to common people, especially the poor and depressed ones. However, Ramakrishna Brahmananda *Ashram* in Trivandrum has a praiseworthy role in the field of health care. In 1937, a dispensary was established at Sasthamangalam in Trivandrum in the name of the Ramakrishna mission by Rao Bahadur K. Raman Thampi, who was formerly director of the Medical Department of the Government of Travancore. He purchased a small house with two rooms for this purpose; one room was used for dispensary and the other was used as Ramakrishna shrine. It was the beginning of the Ramakrishna Ashram General Hospital, which was a landmark in the history of health care system under private initiative. Under this hospital, later on, six mini health centres were opened: Nettayam, Oonnanpara, Cheriyaconni, Anacode, Kizhar, and Vavode to extend medical services to the most poor and the neediest.

It is also remarkable that the mission organized Baby Show and documentary cinema on public health care on various occasions. For example, during the time of rural and industrial exhibition held at Trichur in 1939, there was a baby show that consisted of 79 babies divided into three groups as babies under three years, two years and one year. Prizes were given to the babies as judged by physicians. There was also a documentary movie on health care on the occasion.[27] The objective of this baby show and cinema was to generate awareness among the common people about good health practices, particularly in the case of child health care.

d) Prabuddha Keralam and other Publications

Although messages of Sri Ramakrishna started to get published in printed Malayalam as early as 1910, the necessity of a regular publication was revealed on the occasion of the visit of Swami Nirmalananda to Thiruvalla *ashram* in 1915. Hence, Swami suggested the publication of *Prabuddha Keralam* magazine and entrusted his disciple Velukutty Menon to bring out the work. On 17 October 1915, the first issue of the magazine was released in Kollam (Quilon).[28] Swami Niranjananda (pre-*sannyasa* name N.S. Pandala) became the editor of the magazine. In 1918, its printing and publication were shifted to Trivandrum under the editorship of K. Padmanabhan Thampi, who later accepted *sannyasa* and became Swami Paramananda. For a short period from 1933 to 1935, it was published from Ottappalam, and again brought to Trivandrum in 1935. Meanwhile the Kalady *ashram* had been publishing a magazine called *Amruthavani*. As both these publications possessed common objectives—to spread the message of Sri Ramakrishna and Vivekananda—the authorities of the mission decided to amalgamate *Amruthavani* with *Prabuddha Keralam* for more effective spiritual and intellectual enlightenment of Keralites. From 1955 onwards, new *Prabuddha Keralam* with an opening message "Amruthavani" was brought out from Kalady.

In 1964, a special issue of *Prabuddha Keralam* as part of Vivekananda centenary programs was printed and published from Puranattukara *ashram*, Trichur. Swami Ishwarananda was the editor of the magazine in the beginning phase of publication. Subsequently, Puranattukara became the centre of printing and publishing of *Prabuddha Keralam*; still it goes on regularly and perfectly enlightening the Kerala society with 5,500 subscribers. At present the editor of the magazine is Swami Sadbhavananda.

In addition to *Prabuddha Keralam*, the Puranattukara *ashram* brought out twenty-four books in Malayalam dealing with teachings of Sri Ramakrishna, Karma yoga, Raja yoga, Bhakti yoga, Jnana yoga, education, speeches of Vivekananda, Vedanta, Christianity and other subjects and books for children. The Kalady *ashram* also published several books on similar themes. Digitalized publications are also available nowadays in the *ashrams*. These publications had an important role in the spiritual and intellectual enlightenment of the people of Kerala.

e) Disaster Relief Activities

Another field of service, though not very prominent, was taking care of the people during the time of natural disasters like floods that often occurred in Kerala. The origin of Ramakrishna *ashram* at Puranattukara itself was in fact linked with the flood relief activities of the mission in 1924. The *ashram* in Quilandy was the centre of Ramakrishna Mission's relief work during the period of 1924 floods in Malabar. In the 1940s, when there was cholera and famine, the Quilandy *ashram* again stood in the frontline for relief services in different places of Malabar. Other *ashrams* also undertook such relief activities as and when they were required in different parts of Kerala. The report of the mission in 1941 stated as follows:

> Immediately on receipt of the first news of the havoc, workers of the Ramakrishna Mission proceeded to the affected area and began organizing distribution of rice and building materials from two centres, one at Cochin State at Trichur and the other in Valapad in British Malabar, reaching a radius of five miles from each centre. During the period of one and a half month up to July 13 (subsequent figures not yet received), the relief party working from two centres gave relief to 17,476 persons of 2645 families in 37 villages. [29]

The report also said "the public are fully aware of the services rendered by the Ramakrishna Mission in the past in this direction... and they know that every pie handed over to the mission will be well spent."[30]

Swami Ranganathananda: Gift of Kerala to the Ramakrishna Mission

This study on the role of Ramakrishna Mission in Kerala is not an exhaustive one, but it may look unfinished without a note on Swami Ranganathananda, who became the President of Ramakrishna Mission in 1998. Sankarankutty, his pre-*sannyasa* name, was born in

Trikkur village near Trichur in 1908. Attracted by the teachings of Vivekananda, he joined the *ashram* in Mysore in 1928 and initiated as a *sannyasi* in 1933. He was appointed the President of the Karachi centre of the mission in 1942 and remained there until 1948. During this period, L.K. Advani was a frequent visitor of the ashram to listen his discourse on the Upanishads and *Bhagavat Gita*. Advani said that Ranganathananda was a "great influence" during his formative years. According to Advani at Karachi, Mohammed Ali Jinnah had once listened to Ranganathananda's lecture on Islam and Prophet Mohammed and said, "Now I know how a true Muslim should be."[31] After his return from Karachi he served as a secretary at the Delhi centre of the mission from 1949 to1962, then as secretary of the Ramakrishna Mission Institute of Culture, Kolkata until 1967. He was elected to the post of vice-president of Ramakrishna *Mutt* and Mission in 1988. And in 1998 he became the President of the Mission.

Swami Ranganathananda traversed the length and breadth of India spreading the true message of V*edanta* and *Sanatana Dharma*. He devoted his entire life to the Ramakrishna Mission and worked with compassion and generosity for the liberation of the masses of India. Like Swami Vivekananda, he visited foreign countries–the USA, European countries, Australia, Singapore, Russia, Iran–to spread the message of Indian spiritual culture and ideals of V*edanta*. There are about 50 books authored by Swami. *Eternal Values for a Changing Society* and commentaries on the messages of Bhagavat Gita and Upanishads are his outstanding contributions. Though Ranganathananda was chosen by Government of India for Padma Vibhushan Award in 2000, he declined the award as it was conferred on him in his individual capacity and not for the mission. But Swami accepted the Indira Gandhi Award for National Integration in 1987 and the Gandhi Peace Prize in February 1999 as both were conferred on the Ramakrishna Mission for its praiseworthy contributions in respective realms.

Conclusion

Swami Vivekananda's visit to Kerala exposed its social conditions to the rest of India and he underlined the urgency of social reform and education to nurture humanitarian values. Although the teachings of Sri Ramakrishna and the messages of Swami Vivekananda began to spread in Kerala by the dawn of the twentieth century, activities of Ramakrishna Mission formally started with the establishment of Ramakrishna Ashram at Haripad in 1913. Social reform activities, especially program for the social uplift of the Harijans and fight against caste system, educational services with emphasis on Harijans and other downtrodden sections, and health care were the predominant areas of the activities of the mission. It is noteworthy that the message of Vivekananda and reform programs of the Ramakrishna Mission gave a boost to the work of social reformers in twentieth century Kerala. The *misra-bhojanam* at Haripad and Sri Ramakrishna Jayanthi march comprising outcaste from the precincts of Subramanya temple at Haripad were prelude to the *misra-bhojanam* and temple entry *satyagrahas* organized by later day social reformers of Kerala. Educational activities undertaken by Ramakrishna ashrams at Calicut, Trichur and Kalady and the health care programs of the *ashram* at Trivandrum are exemplary services of the Ramakrishna Mission to humanity.

In fact, the principal objective of the Ramakrishna Mission was to achieve social liberty and equality for all and to foster true spirituality in all. Services of the mission demonstrate love of men and love of God. It reflects what Swami Vivekananda wrote to Alasinga on 27 October 1894: "I believe in God and I believe in Man. I believe in helping the miserable, I believe in going even to hell to save others⬜"[32] He wrote to Swami Akhandananda, on 15 June 1897: "It is the heart, the heart that conquers, not the brain. Books and learning, yoga and meditation and illumination—all are but dust compared with love. It is love that gives you supernatural powers, love that gives you Bhakti, love that gives you illumination, and love again, that leads to emancipation."[33] It is this ideal of love of men, particularly of the poor, the depressed and the outcaste that formed the foundation of the Ramakrishna Mission. It is again this ideal of love that leads to the attainment of unity of all men and women in true religion. Finally to put in epigrammatic sense, the Ramakrishna Mission helped the social, intellectual, spiritual empowerment and enlightenment of the common people, particularly the downtrodden ones of Kerala.

REFERENCES AND NOTES

1. Cited in Swami Prbhananda, *The Early History of Ramakrishna Movement*, Chennai: Ramakrishna Math, 2005, p. 354

2. Romain Rolland, *The Life of Ramakrishna*, Kolkata: Advaita Ahram, reprint 2007, pp.169-192, 207, 216-17.

3. Swami Ranganathananda, "Swami Vivekananda: His Life and Mission", *Vivekananda Centenary Souvenir, 1963*, Trichur, 1963, pp. 27-28.

4. 'Kerala' in this paper may be understood as a common linguistic and cultural area comprising Travancore and Cochin and Malabar before and after 1956.

5. Interview with Swami Vivekananda, *The Madras Mail*, 6 February 1897, in Sankari Prasad Basu, ed., *Swami Vivekananda in Contemporary Indian News, 1893-1902*, Kolkata: Ramakrishna Mission Institute of Culture, 2007, pp. 552-53.

6. Rajeev Iringalakkuda, *Swami Vivekanandanum Keralavum* (Malayalam), Thiruvananthapuram: the State Institute of Languages, 2012, pp. 34-35. Some of the information about early Ramakrishna *ashrams* in this discussion is drawn from this book.

7. V.K.A (Vedanta Kesari Archives), Report of Ramakrishna Mission Work in Kerala, 1924-25, p. 314

8. Rajeev, *Swami Vivekanandanum Keralavum*, p. 37.

9. A few *ashrams* like the one at Dharmmadam founded by Swami Nirmalananda, one in Kajiranpara, another one at Aroor etc do not function nowadays.

10. *The Complete Works of Swami Vivekananda*, vol. III, Kolkata: Advaita Ashrama, 2009, pp. 294-95. See also the same collection vol. IV, p. 342, where it has been said: "In Malabar a Chandala is not allowed to pass through the same street as a high caste man, but let him become a Mohammedan or Christian, he will be immediately allowed to go anywhere." 'Malabar' historically refers to Kerala, though under the colonial rule it was a district under Madras Presidency in North Kerala,

11. Editorial, *The Madras Times*, 27 August 1895, , in Sankari Prasad Basu, ed., *Swami Vivekananda in Contemporary Indian News*, vol. II, p. 397.

12 Vivekananda interviewed, *The Madras Mail*, 6 February 1897, in Sankari Prasad Basu, ed., *Swami Vivekananda in Contemporary Indian News*, vol. II, p. 551.

13 *The Life of Swami Vivekananda*, by His Eastern and Western Disciples, Kolkata: Advaita Ashram, 11ᵗʰ reprint, 2011, p.321.

14 Then Vivekananda told him: "Why do you go after the Brahmins? Find out some good noble person from among your own people and follow him." Thus Palpu took his advice seriously and discovered such a person in Sri Narayanana Guru, the prominent leader of social reform movement in Kerala. *Ibid.*, p. 320.

15 For details of Swami Vivekananda's visit to Kerala see *The Life of Vivekananda*, vol.1, Kolkata, 2011, pp. 325-340. V.M. Korath, "Vivekananda Swamikal Keralathil" in *Vivekananda Satakaprasasthi, 1963*, Trichur, 1963, pp. 120-26

16 Rajeev, *Swami Vivekanandanum Keralavum*, p. 35

17 *Ibid.*, p. 36

18 Report in *The Hindu*, 12 March, 1897 in Sankari Prasad Basu, ed., *Swami Vivekananda in Contemporary Indian News, 1893-1902*, vol. I, Kolkata, 2007, p.300

19 Vivekanada interviewed by the correspondent of *The Madras Mail* in the train during his journey from Chingelpet to Madras, 6 February 1897, Sankari Prasad Basu, *Swami Vivekananda in Contemporary Indian News, 1893-1902*, vol. II, Kolkata, 2007, p.549.

20 *The Complete Works of Swami Vivekananda*, vol. 7, p. 508, Vivekananda to Shuddhananda, 11 July 1897.

21 Vivekananda's Speech "The Future of India" in *The Madras Mail* 15 February 1897, Sankari Prasad Basu, *Swami Vivekananda in Contemporary Indian News, 1893-1902*, vol. II, Kolkata, 2007, p.569.

22 Vivekanada interviewed, *The Madras Mail*, 6 February 1897 ibid. p. 551.

23 Thrissur *Mutt* details from V.K. Archives, Report, February-March, 1936, p. 470.

24 *Ibid.* The Tuskegee Institute in Alabama was founded and developed by African-American educator Booker T. Washington for the blacks in the USA in 1881. At present it is the Tuskegee University.

68

25 V.K. Archives, Report of Sri Ramakrishna Ashram, The Vilangans, 1946.

26 V.K. Archives, Report of Sri Ramakrishna Gurukula and Industrial Exhibition, May, 1939, p. 40.

27 *Ibid.*

28 An unpublished manuscript, "Sreeramakrishna Prathanavum Prabuddha Keralavum (Mal)", available at Puranattukara *ashram* has been used for discussing the history of the magazine.

29 V.K. Archives, Report on Ramakrishna Mission Cyclone Relief in Malabar and Cochin, August, 1941, p. 159

30 *Ibid.*

31 Swami Ranganathananda, Wikipedia

32 Cited in *The Life of Vivekananda*, p. 557.

33 *The Complete Works of Swami Vivekananada*, vol. 6, pp. 400-01

❧ Chapter 8 ❧

Swami Vivekananda and the Upliftment of Women in the Society

Christina Kokila. W.

Asst. Prof. of History
Madras Christian College,
Tambaram, Chennai-59

"There is no chance of the welfare of the world unless the condition of women is improved. It is not possible for a bird to fly on one wing" – Swami Vivekananda.

During the Vedic times there was great respect for women amounting to worship. It started to deplore during the later Vedic period. After the invasion of the Arabs and the entry of Turks in India, their condition started to deteriorate even more and so during the time of the British rule. The Indian society in the nineteenth century had fallen into a stage of degeneration after centuries of Afghan and Mughal and then, the British rule. The British rule, specially, had created widespread poverty and hunger, and the propaganda of these missionaries had created a sense of insecurity among the people about their traditional customs and beliefs. Faced with these threats, the caste ridden society has retreated into a shell, and in order to protect them from this attack became more orthodox and repressive. At this crucial point, rose a number of important reformers like Raja Ram Mohan Roy, Swami Dayananada Saraswati and Swami Vivekananda. They strived ceaselessly to reform the Indian society, and in doing so raised a new voice of pan nationalism. They were thus vanguards of Freedom Movement.[1] The first voice of protest was not so much against the political exploitation by the British but against their moral exploitation of the Indian Society and this was to guide and provide the unique feature of the Indian Freedom struggle.[2]

Swami Vivekananda's position was unique. He was in close touch with the Hindu religion and with the Western Philosophy. He was thus able to take up the best features of both in his work and attempt to fuse them in his dream of the future. The message he preached in India was not the renunciation and mysticism that he used to hear. Instead he cried for work—work for the downtrodden and the poor of the country, work to revitalize the society as a whole. Strength was his message to Indians—physical strength, moral strength, strength to work for others. He rallied against the weaknesses that had crept into the society and preached self control for the young.

Swami Vivekananda was one of the most enduring icons of the rise of Indian nationalism in modern India. He was one among the first generation leaders who raised the voice of Indian Nationality. He was an intensely religious man who lived a life immersed in spirituality.[3] Vivekananda repeatedly told that India's downfall was largely due to her negligence of women. The great images of Brahmavadinis like Maitreyi and Gargi of the Upanishad age and women missionaries like Sanghamitra carrying Buddha's message to Syria and Macedonia all were laying buried deep due to millennium of foreign domination.

Vivekananda strongly reasoned the cause of such degradation of Indian woman. "The Principal reason why our race has so degenerated is that we had no respect for these living images of Shakti". Manu says, "Where women are respected, there the Gods delight, and where they are not, there all work and efforts come to naught." There is no hope of rise for that family or country where they live in sadness. Thus Swami was particularly worried about the degradation of Indian women.

Vivekananda strongly believed that there is a huge difference in the attitude of Indian men and their western counterparts. Indian men believe that the women are born to please them. The real Shakti-worshipper is he who knows that God is the omnipresent force in the Universe, and sees in women the manifestation of that force. In America, men look upon their women in this light and treat their women as well can be desired, and hence they are so prosperous, so learned, so free and so energetic.[4]

Are Indian men family oriented and have a deep set of values embedded in them since childhood? It has lot to do with their upbringing in their family. In India, little boys are told that they are stronger than girls—that sparks off a dominating streak in them, that stays with them throughout their lives and manifests in various ways, be it teasing a woman on the road or treating the wife like a sex toy. It is the value learnt at home that affects through subtle messages parents often indicate that the girls will be going to another household, while the boys would learn and inherit the family's wealth. Naturally they grow up believing that they are superior to women and may mistreat their parents later. Why can't we tell little boys to be more sensitive towards girls rather than feeding their brains about such lame notion. There is no chance for the welfare of the world unless the condition of women is improved. Swami Vivekananda said, "It is very difficult to understand why this country has so much indifference made between men and women, whereas the Vedanta declares that one and the same conscious self is present in all beings. You always criticize the women, but what have you done for their enlistment?"

Swami Vivekananda glorified Indian women of the past for their great achievements as leaders in various walks of life. He proudly states that "Women in statesmanship, managing territories, government, even making war, have proved themselves equal to men, if not superior. In India there is no doubt that whenever there was an opportunity they proved they have as much ability as men. They keep their moral standards, which is innate in their nature. And thus as Governors and rulers of their state, they prove that they are far superior to men—John Stuart Mill mentions this fact".[5] Swami Vivekananda was a monk who at one time saw women as an obstacle. However on realizing the highest truth he saw no distinction between sexes and saw in women the presence of the Divine Mother.

For Swami Vivekananda, it was really difficult to understand why in this country (India) so much difference was made between men and women, whereas the Vedanta declares that one and the same conscious self is present in all beings. You will criticize that women but say what have you done for their uplift? Writing down Smiritis, etc., and binding them by hard rules, the men have turned women into manufacturing machines! If you do not raise the women, who are living embodiment of the Divine Mother, don't think that you have any other way to rise.

Swami Vivekananda once rightly questioned "In what scriptures do you find statements that women are not competent for knowledge and devotion?" In the period of degeneration, when the priest made the other castes incompetent for the study of the Vedas or Upanishadic age, Maitreyi, Gargi and other ladies of revered memory have taken places of Rishis through their skill in discussing about Brahman. In an assembly of a thousand Brahmans who were all erudite in the Vedas, Gargi boldly challenges Yajnavalkya in a discussion about Brahman. Since such ideal women were entitled to spiritual knowledge, why shall not the women have privilege now? What had happened once can certainly happen again. History repeats itself. All nations have attained greatness by paying proper respect to women. That country and that nation which do not respect women have never become great, nor will ever be in future. The principal reason why your race has so much degenerated is that you have no respect for these living images of Shakti. Manu says "Where women are respected, there the Gods are delight: and where they are not, there all works and efforts come to naught". There is no hope of rise for that family or country where there is no estimation of women, where they live in sadness.

Swami Vivekananda rightly observed that the condition of women in Mughal ruled and British ruled India was deplorable. In the period of degeneration when the priest made other caste incompetent to study the Vedas, they deprived the women also of all their rights. As found in the Vedic and Upanishad age, Maitreyi, Gargi and other ladies of revered memory have taken the place of Rishis.

Swami Vivekananda was of the firm opinion that women should be put in positions of power to solve their own problems in their own way. The status of women in a society would reflect the importance and value of women in a nation.

Swami Vivekananda believed that women who mould the next generation and the destiny of the country should be honoured and respected. In Vivekananda's educational scheme for India, the uplift of women and the masses received the highest priority. The idea of perfect womanhood is perfect independence.

Vivekananda declared that the western ideal of womanhood is wife, while the eastern ideal is mother. "The very peculiarity of Indian Women which they have developed and which is their ideal of life is that of the mother..." An educated nation that would look upon God as Mother has learnt to invest its view of woman with the utmost tenderness and reverence. Swami Vivekananda is the first monk to uphold and do work for the freedom and equality of women and realizing her importance for the functioning of home and society.

It is the strong belief of Swami Vivekananda that if women are raised, their children will by their noble actions glorify the name of the country: then will culture, knowledge, power and devotion awake in the country.

With five hundred men, the conquest of India might take fifty years: but with as many women not more than a few weeks. All nations have attained greatness by paying proper respect to women. That country and that nation which do not respect women have never become great, nor will ever be in future, amen.

REFERENCES

1. Avinashalingam, T.S. 1974, Educational Philosophy of Swami Vivekananda, 3rd ed Coimbatore

2. Sengupta, S.C. 1984, Swami Vivekananda and Indian Nationalism, Calcutta: Shishu Sahitya Samsad.

3. Teachings of Swami Vivekananda, Kolkata: Advaita Ashrama.

4. Nivedita, Sister.1999, The Master as I saw him. 9th ed., 12th printing, Calcutta: Udbodhan Office.

5. Singh S.K. Religious and moral Philsosphy of Swami Vivekananda. Patna: Janaki Prakashan.

6. Burke, M.L. 1984. Swami Vivekananda in the West: new discoveries, 6 vols.Calcutta: Advaita Ashrama.

Chapter 9

Thoughts of Swami Vivekananda in the Present Scenario

Dr.N. Dhanalakshmi

Asst. Prof & Head i/c
School of History and Tourism Studies
Tamil Nadu Open University
No.577, Anna Salai
Saidapet, Chennai-600015.

The UNESCO is committed to contribute to peace and security by promoting collaboration among the nations through education, science and culture in order to further universal respect for justice, for the rule of law and for the human rights and fundamental freedoms which are affirmed for the people of the world, without distinction of race, sex, language or religion, by the Charter of the United Nations. But, even more than five decades before the establishment of UNESCO, the great visionary, Swami Vivekananda had precisely set the same ideals as the goal of his Mission. His commitment to universalism and tolerance is active identification with humanity as a whole. He showed remarkable concern for the poor and the destitute people. The Mission he established in India and which has now spread all over the world is working to reduce poverty and eliminate discrimination among the different segments of the society. In fact, this is the greatest challenge we face today. Both the Mission and the UNESCO place the human being at the centre of their efforts in their development. Both place tolerance at the top of their agenda for building peace and democracy. Both recognize the variety of the human cultures and societies as an essential aspect of the common heritage.[1]

Let us now analyse how Swamiji's teachings are relevant for the modern times. Society is only a collection of individuals. Society reflects man's nature in a collective way. If we analyse the social developments in the last couple of centuries, one observes a very important change in man's attitude to others, we see a steady fall in ethical standards in society. Corruption, greed, one-upmanship, deception, suppression, oppression, and denial resulting in total lack of social commitment in our dealings and reckless disregard for the inconveniences caused by our actions to others in society have all been on the rise. On the other hand, there is steady rise in India's literacy, which is equated with education by our government.

Of course, present education has resulted in lots of technical advancements. Man has succeeded in going to the Moon and hopes to live on the planet Mars soon. True education, however, should be able to make man land in his neighbour's living room with a smile on his/her face to care and share. That has not happened with our education today. On the contrary, our present education has made man the greatest enemy of another man. We live in apartments today keeping us apart and have stopped living in homes built with universal love. We live in the space age, thanks to science, which has resulted in increasing the space between man and man! Education should inculcate in this era of nuclear arms and biological weapons, the social conscience, which would bring man and man together. Although technology has shrunk the world into a small neighbourhood, mankind's social conscience is yet to broaden to make it a brotherhood.[2]

Nearly 700-800 million young men and women are looking for higher educational facilities in the next fifty odd years. Voltaire, the great French thinker, once wrote: "While we were hunter-gathers, roaming the forests, India had some of the world's greatest universities which attracted students from all over the civilized world to acquire wisdom". According to Vivekananda himself, perfection means achieving the stage where one stands on one's legs, well-equipped to win the struggles of life with a spirit of philanthropy and the courage of a lion. He emphasised that education is the process of bringing out in a human being the capacity, the propensity and the capability of self-development and self-empowerment in order to be self-reliant with a spirit of philanthropy and courage.

In respect of the secular values, Swamiji believes that 'Education is not the amount of information that is put into your brain and runs riot there, undigested, all your life. We must have life-building, man-making, character-making assimilation of ideas'. So, according to him, at the end of education, all training should be on man-making.[3] Education should let human beings grow. What the country wants for that, he says, are 'muscles of iron and nerves of steel'. First of all, our young men and women must be strong. Religion will come afterwards. This is the special characteristic of Vivekananda. How true it is in the present scenario.[4]

This brings us to the next idea—the issue of moral and ethical education. Explaining the essence of religion, Swami Vivekananda said, 'Religion is not in books, nor in theories, nor in dogmas, nor in talking, not even in reasoning. It is being and becoming'. Alas! the earth is as much, if not more, filled with violence and fanaticism today as it was then. What happened on 11 September 2001 in New York and on 26 November 2008 in Mumbai? Those were cruel demonstrations of the continued misuse and misinterpretation of religion. The events of the world remind us of Vivekananda's words, 'The noblest words of peace that the world has ever heard have come from men on the religious plane, and the bitterest denunciation that the world has ever known has been uttered by religious men.'[5]

The world today is passing through great crisis. There is a great necessity therefore to stress the importance that the Swami gave to moral education for the cultivation of peace, a spirit of acceptance and inclusiveness. He was skeptical about the efficacy of dry intellectual training, which in most cases churns out irreligious persons. It is one of the evils of the Western civilization, he said, for mere intellectual education that does not take care of the heart only makes man ten times more selfish.[6] We know about the recent financial crisis all over the world. The brains behind the whole scheme were all highly educated professionals who cheated the world, and who did not have the heart to feel the misery of the people they were cheating. We are also aware how the market dominated society fuels the greed for unlimited material progress.

There are other problems such as deforestation, global warming, water and air pollution which are direct consequences of heedless industrial development. The tsunami was a bitter lesson for us. The irregular climatic changes, droughts and recurring floods are all affecting our day-to-day lives severely and that is because of uncaring industrialization. The development of biotechnology and benefits, bioinformatics have brought along some problems of gene cloning, surrogate motherhood and invasion on privacy.[7]

The phenomenon of computerization is now affecting even our private lives. Of course, there are good effects of all these but unregulated use of the devices of modern science and technology can wreak havoc in our lives. If we do not care to connect basic ethics with technological progress we are bound to usher in an era of barbarism with a human face and destroy the earth.[8]

So, how do we face the situation? How will we give ethical education to the terrorists? This is a big challenge now, because the terrorists have also been created by education. Like religion, there has been gross misuse of education when the Talibans are trained to terrorize people. In some parts of the world women are trained to become suicide bombers. What is the solution then? Should we hate education? Certainly not. We have to transform this 'hate education' attitude to 'love education' outlook. Is it impossible? I do not think so because education has tremendous capacity to transform the human mind. If it can be done in the negative way, we can also do it in a positive way. But to do that, we must have the political will, commitment, and an institutional framework which Vivekananda's ideas provide. He said, 'In a conflict between the heart and the brain, follow the heart.' Dwelling on the aspect of ethical education, he said that religions of the world are not contradictory or antagonistic, they are but various faces of one eternal religion. 'Our watchword, then, will be acceptance, and not exclusion'.

Women in India were far behind men in the field of education when Swamiji lived. Now the situation has somewhat improved but much remains to be done. Observing the state of women's education in India, Swamiji lamented that he could not understand why so much difference was made between men and women, especially when Vedanta declared that one and the same Self was present in all beings. He quoted Manu to assert that daughters should be supported and educated with as much care and attention as the sons. This discrimination is made in every part of the world even now. Swamiji therefore demanded forcefully that women must be put in a position so that they could solve their problems in their own way. Why not? He rightly pointed out unerringly that it was only in the homes of educated and pious mothers that great men and women were born.[9] Vivekananda's thinking on women's education is more significant today when, in the name of religion, the women in some countries are deprived not only of education but also of health care and other basic human rights.

Swami Vivekananda always believed that the development of a nation is not possible without real education. According to him, development of good personality in every human being is very essential in case of nation building. Morality has become a complicated issue in the multi-cultural world we live in today. Morality describes the principles that govern our behaviour. Without these principles in place, societies cannot survive for long. In today's world, morality is frequently thought of as belonging to a particular religious point of view, but by definition, we see that this is not the case. According to Vivekananda, love is the highest goal of religion. Man should imbibe love for all and hatred for none.[10] According to him education without character is like a flower without fragrance. An education system that doesn't recognize this can be self-defeatist at the best.

Swamiji lived in the 19th century. But his statements and his message are very much relevant even today! Frankly speaking, his ideas are even more necessary today to be practiced and realized than they were during his time, not only by the Indians but also by the people of the whole world. Let us, as he said, "awake and stop not until the goal is achieved".

REFERENCES

1. Revisiting Educational Thoughts and Action of Swami Vivekananda by Bikas C. Sanyal, Bulletin of the Ramakrishna Mission Institute of Culture, January 11 September 2012.

2. Vivekananda, Conquering the Internal Nature Advaita, Ashrama, Kolkata, 2006.

3. Vivekananda, S. My India, The India Eternal, The Ramakrishna Mission Institutes of Culture, Kolkata, 1993.

4. Life and Philosophy of Swami Vivekananda, Belur Math, 1989.

5. Vivekananda, Conversation and Dialogues Vol. 5

6. Swami Vivekananda a role model for the youth, *The Hindu* (Chennai) 24 November 2009.

7. Bharathi. K.S. The Political thought of Swami Vivekananda, New Delhi Concept Publishing Company 1998.

8. Majumdar, R.C. Swami Vivekananda-A Historical Review, Advaita Ashrama, 2000.

9. Nikilananda, Swami Vivekananda A Biography Advaita Ashrama, Kolkata, 1964.

10. The Complete works of Swami Vivekanada Advaita Ashrama, Kolkata 1994, Vol 4.

Chapter 10

Swami Vivekananda and his Idea of Social Service

Dr. E. Devabalane

Asst. Professor of Tourism
Department of Tourism
Tagore Arts College
Puducherry-605008

Introduction

Swami, an agnostic-turned-monk, accomplished in his life span of 39 years what is not probably possible for anyone living even for a couple of centuries. His worldwide view and success in the western world revived India's self esteem in the context of the depressed mood of enslavement. He is a combined personality of Buddha, Mahavira, Adi Shankara, Ramanuja, and Chaitanya in a manner of syncretism. He is also a great musician even as a teenager, attracting hundreds of people to his singing, a tradition which he continued throughout his life. He admires the works of Leo Tolstoy and Max Mueller and practised their ideas in his life. Most of his ideas on religion are radical in nature. He once declared "I do not know the 30 crore deities of our pantheon, but I know the millions of my fellowmen suffering who are my Gods to be served". He epitomised this sentiment on the lines **Nara Seva is Narayana Seva.** [Service to Man is Service to God].[38]

Objective of the Study

To know about Swami Vivekananda and his idea about social service.

To know about the types of service to be practised by the youth.

To know about the social service projects and the principles to be followed.

Significance and Method of Study;

The method adopted in this study is through the secondary sources. The intention to work on this particular area is due to the significance of Swami Vivekananda and his contribution to social service for rejuvenating the young minds particularly in India. The secondary sources include journals, books, periodicals, diaries, thesis and other electronic resource materials.

Social Service to the Masses

Swamiji, did not believe in salvation by constantly running away from the world to meditate in caves, he believed that such enlightenment was only a means to serve his fellowmen. So he created an Order of monk at the Ramakrishna Mutt and Mission, who dedicated his youthful life to the upliftment of the downtrodden through education, healthcare, and other social activities. There he laid a strong foundation for the communal and religious harmony, expanding the principles of his guru and demonstrated the idea of social service to the masses. Swami Vivekananda had a plan of work for social service for the masses of this country. He was aware of the difficulties of adult education in a poor country. He pointed out that with the present colossal poverty with the majority of people living in squalor,

---

38   T.S.Avinashilingam,"Education Philosophy of Swami Vivekananda", Sri Ramakrishna Mission Vidyalaya, Coimbatore, 1997. p145

dirt, and malnutrition, the first thing to give them was employment and the wherewithal to get at least two square meals a day. He said to the poor, providing food is the first step to Godliness. Therefore, adult education should not be merely literacy but must consist in improving the capacity of those taught and quality of their work in agriculture, industry, and in the art of living. Swamiji thus foresaw the need for functional literacy movement to give a purposive slant to education so as to raise their capacity for work and achievement. He said;

Then only will India awake when hundreds of large-hearted men and women giving up all desire of enjoying the luxuries of life, will exert themselves to their utmost, for the wellbeing of the millions of their countrymen who are gradually sinking lower and lower in the vortex of destitution and ignorance. Good motives, sincerity and infinite love can conquer the world. One single soul possessed of these virtues can destroy the dark designs of millions of hypocrites and brutes.[39]

In his Karma Yoga, Swami Vivekananda has expounded the basic attitudes required of a good social worker: "while it is a great privilege for all of us to be allowed to do anything for the world, let us also remember that in helping the world we really help ourselves". The world will always continue to be a mixture of good and evil. Our duty is to sympathise with the weak and to love even the wrongdoers. The world is a grand moral gymnasium wherein we all have to take exercise so as to become stronger spiritually[40].

Any work that is done with the least selfish motive instead of making us free forges one more chain for our feet. So the only way is to give up the fruits of work and be unattached to them.

The Karma Yogi asks why you require any motive to work other than the inborn love of freedom. Be beyond the common worldly motives. "To work you have the right; but not to the fruits thereof". Man can train himself to know and to practise that, says the Karma Yogi. When the idea of doing good becomes a part of his very being,

39 S.Krishnaswamy, "A Man among Men" The Hindu, Friday September 21, 2012, p-4

40 T.S.Avinashilingam, "Education Philosophy of Swami Vivekananda", Sri Ramakrishna Mission Vidyalaya, Coimbatore, 1997.p146

then he will not seek for any motive outside. Let us do good because it is good to do good.[41]

Idea of Service

Today independent India has a value system entirely different from that of the past. We call ourselves proudly that we moved from traditional to knowledge based society where ultimately money-making is the single-minded aim. But the young minds should realize their responsibilities and ensure to make ours as an egalitarian society by providing social service to the masses and to protect our values.

Swamiji addressed the issue by simplifying the whole problem of existence. He made national reconstruction with the ideals of **Tyaga** and **Seva** the most important purpose of living for the young. The transience of human achievement and the impermanence of material wealth were of critical consideration to this thinking and made his way of life a 'spiritual pursuit'. He attempted to show us a higher reason to live, a higher ideal to live for a higher state to reach within the limitations and boundaries of a human existence. He wanted our youth to have an ability to 'feel'. He wanted that feeling for our downtrodden and the poor which would make us sleepless and make our heads reel and our hearts stop. In doing so, he assured us that an indomitable power would come to us and we will be able to throw away all our self-concerns and place ourselves as servants of society and use our inner energy and will to transcend the problems of our human relations. Swamiji, insisted the important qualification to our youth that is the wonderful ability to 'feel'. Swami gave this potent mantra, i.e., the power of 3p's—purity, patience, and perseverance. These three magic words were the essential qualities that every young Indians desiring to do social service needs to possess. 'Purity' in thoughts, words and deeds, 'Patience' to understand the dynamics of Indian society and community, and 'Perseverance' to understand the realities of social, economic and political diversity of our country. Hence he called upon the youth to build mental energies as well as the physical to face the challenges as a social worker. To quote him:

---

41   T.S.Avinashilingam, "Education Philosophy of Swami Vivekananda", Sri Ramakrishna Mission Vidyalaya, Coimbatore, 1997.p147

All good work has to go through three stages. First comes ridicule, then the stage of opposition and finally comes acceptance.[42]

Stages of Service

He emphasised three types of service to humanity that one can do. The first is the physical—taking care of the human body and undertaking activities to ameliorate human physical suffering, orphanages, old age homes, hospitals. The next service was the intellectual—running schools, colleges, awareness and empowerment programmes. The highest level of service is spiritual. He clearly, wanted the youth to undertake these activities not merely for the betterment of society but for the evolution and growth of the person undertaking the same. He saw the means of serving society leading on to the end of spiritual growth of the person doing it. And he beautifully advised us to 'Serve God in man'—the highest of his philosophy so elegantly and simply packed into one statement in a lucid language that is attractive and achievable by the youth. Hence his ideas of service looks within the reach of each one of us but makes it so emotionally appealing and highly motivating to perform such activities. He needs to ensure that his physical, mental, emotional, social, and psychological faculties are well tuned to the work ahead. One has to understand that social service does not automatically translate as giving up all the worldly responsibilities. In fact it begins with arousing one's social conscience and transforming it into practical social actions. One needs to be pragmatic and keep one's needs and limitations in mind before embarking on any such activity in the society.[43]

While undergoing social service projects one has to remember the basic principles:

. The projects should meet the genuine needs of the community or the group they are meant to serve and their value should be apparent to the community as well as the workers.

42 N.Balu. "Swami Vivekananda's message of social service for the youth of India, Balu musings, p 4, Feb 12, 2011
43 N.Balu. "Swami Vivekananda's message of social service for the youth of India, Balu musings, p 5, Feb 12, 2011

- Local community should be given an opportunity to participate in the planning and execution of the work.

- Unskilled participants' also have the opportunity to work.

- Leaders should have adequate skill and training, practical and theoretical knowledge in various functions to be performed.

Program should be well balanced to sustain the interest of the youths and their schemes.

Conclusion

Let me tell you in conclusion a few words about one man who actually carried this teaching of Karma Yoga into practise. That man is Buddha. He is the one man who ever carried this into perfect practise, who said, "I do not care to know your various theories about God. What is the use of discussing all the subtle doctrines about the soul? Do good and be good. And this will take you to freedom and to whatever there is." This great philosopher, preaching the highest philosophy, yet had the deepest sympathy for the lowest of animals, and never put forth any claims for himself. He was the first who dared to say, "Believe not because some old manuscripts are produced, believe not because it is your national belief, because you have been made to believe it from your childhood; but reason it all out, and after you have analysed it, then, if you find that it will do good to one and all, believe it; live up to it, and help others to live up to it." He works best who works without any motive, neither for money, nor for fame, nor for anything else; and when a man can do that, he will be a Buddha, and out of him will come the power to work in such a manner as will transform the World.[44]

We therefore owe everything to Swami Vivekananda. May his courage, faith, idea, wisdom ever inspire us particularly the youth of India, so that we may keep safe the treasure that we received from the young saint!

44 7.T.S.Avinashilingam, "Education Philosophy of Swami Vivekananda", Sri Ramakrishna Mission Vidyalaya, Coimbatore, 1997.p149

REFERENCES

1. T.S.Avinashilingam, "Education Philosophy of Swami Vivekananda", Sri Ramakrishna Mission Vidyalaya, Coimbatore, 1997.p143-149

2. S.Krishnaswamy, "A Man among Men" The Hindu, Friday September 21,2 012, p-4

3. N.Balu "Swami Vivekananda's message of social service for the youth of India, Balu musings, p 1-6, Feb 12, 2011.

⤳ Chapter 11 ⤳

Swami Vivekananda: A Spiritual Luminary and a Patriotic Saint

Jeedigunta Chalapathi Rao

Assistant Professor
Head of the Department of History
Kasthurba College for Women
Villianur, Puducherry- 605110

Swami Vivekananda was one of the greatest souls ever born in India. He was saint, patriot and philosopher. His indomitable courage, broad vision, spiritual outlook, mature wisdom and deep knowledge blended with an unending spirit of patriotism made him an outstanding personality of India as well as the world. India is justly proud of this great genius. The philosophy of oneness of religion is of his universal appeal and he also believed those who had completely and unreservedly dedicated themselves to the worship of God through service of man. For this vision he started Ramakrishna Mission which stands as a shining example of his lofty ideals, such as humanity, spirituality, and ardent nationalism. He had given importance and suggestions for the development of low caste masses or downtrodden. His teachings helped in revitalising the people of India from Himalayas to

Cape of Comorin, by harmonising all differences and infusing enormous strength in their minds and helping to raise them from stupor, lethargy and despair. His contribution to awaken the people of India to a realisation of their cultural and spiritual heritage is immense. Swami Vivekananda is one of the immortals about whom we should know; about his early life and how he got these virtues.

Early life of Vivekananda

Swami Vivekananda was born as Narendranath in Calcutta, the former capital of British colonial India, on 12th January 1863. He belonged to an aristocratic traditional Bengali Kayastha (a caste Hindus) family. During his childhood, he was fascinated by the wandering ascetics and monks. He showed an inclination towards spirituality and God realisation which stirred him to become an ascetic. In Vivekananda's family there was a precedence of ascetics, his grandfather Durga Charan Datta renounced the world at the age of twenty-five and became a monk[1], probably Vivekananda was also influenced by his grandfather. His father Viswanath Datta was an attorney of Calcutta High Court.[2] Viswanath Datta had a liberal, progressive outlook on social and religious matters.[3] Bhuvaneswari Devi, mother of Vivekananda, was a pious woman. The ascetic attitude of his grandfather, rational approach of his father and the religious temperament of his mother shaped young Vivekananda's thinking and personality.[4] In his later life, Vivekananda often referenced a saying of his mother, "Remain pure all your life; guard your own honour and never transgress the honour of others. Be very tranquil but when necessary harden your heart".[5] Vivekananda had interest and a wide range of scholarship in philosophy, religion, history, the social sciences, arts, literature, and other subjects. He had also interest in the Hindu scriptures such as the *Vedas*, the *Upanishads*, the *Bhagavad Gita*, the *Ramayana*, the *Mahabharata*, and the *Puranas*. He regularly participated in physical exercise, sports, and organizational activities. Even when he was young, he questioned the validity of superstitious customs and discrimination based on caste and refused to accept anything without rational proof and pragmatic test. Later, his guru taught that service to the men is service to the God—to carry this principle, Vivekananda travelled extensively in India for visiting centers of learning, acquainting himself with the diverse religious traditions, different patterns of social life and poverty of India. He developed sympathy on the sufferers and poverty-striken masses and resolved to uplift the nation. During these travels he made acquaintance with all cultures of individuals and stayed with Indians from all walks of life, he also met many scholars, Dewans, Rajas, Hindus, Muslims, Christians, *pariah* workers (Dalit workers) and government officials.[6] In these travels, he tasted the feelings of spirituality, humanity and patriotism.

Vedanta or Spiritual Philosophy of Vivekananda

Some of the outstanding personalities in Indian history who had contributed to the political, cultural and spiritual regeneration of the people had been sanyasins or house holders, who had completely and unreservedly dedicated themselves to the worship of God through service of man—such an enthusiastic man was Swami Vivekananda who voiced the world message of his master, the Message of Prabuddha Bharata, or the 'Awakened India.' Swami Vivekananda "was a strong revivalist force of the last quarter of the 19th century". He was the apostle of Modern Vedantism[7] and preached that the world is not Maya or illusion but a stage in the evolution of mankind towards progress. The closing years of the 19th century had witnessed a period having its uniqueness in the history of India. There were the movements of social and religious revivalism which dug up the buried glories of India's past and brought them out into the limelight of India's reawakened consciousness. All social, religious reform organisations drew their inspiration from the Vedas, Upanishads, past history of India, and they not only tried to awaken India but also give an impetus to the national movement. One of the favourite subjects of these reform movements were the condemnation of caste system and an emphasis on the unity among the Indians. And this made its contribution towards the rise of nationalism. For this approach, the Ramakrishna Mission was formally founded by Vivekananda as a part of socio-religious reform movement for the propagation of Hindu Dharma and spread of patriotic ideas in India. He praised that our sacred motherland is a land of religion and philosophy, the birth place of spiritual giants, the land of renunciation, and that from the most ancient to the most modern times, [8] there has been the highest ideal of life open to man. This is the mother of ethics, sweetness, gentleness and love.

Swami Vivekananda was questioned and pointed out by one of the lay disciples about the difficulty of establishing unity and harmony among the diverse sects in India. Vivekananda replied to the lay disciples with irritation: "Don't come here anymore if you think any task too difficult. Through the grace of the Lord, everything becomes easy of achievement. Your duty is to serve the poor and the distressed without distinction of caste and creed. What business you have to consider the fruits of your action. Your duty is to go on working, and everything will set itself right in time, and work by itself. Swami Vivekananda said that my method of work is to construct, and not to destroy that which already exists....You are all intelligent boys and profess to be my disciples—he asked that what you have done. Couldn't you give away one life for the sake of others?" "Let the reading of Vedanta and the practice of meditation and the like be left for the next life! Let this body go in the service of others and then I shall know you have not come to me in vain!"[9]

The Swami's mission was both national and international. He was a lover of mankind, strove to promote peace and human brotherhood on the spiritual foundation of the Vedanta that was oneness of existence. As a sage of the highest order, Vivekananda had a direct and intuitive experience of reality. He derived his ideas from that reliable source of wisdom and often presented them in the soul-stirring language of poetry. The natural tendency of Vivekananda's mind was to ascend above the world and forget itself in meditation of the absolute like that of his master Ramakrishna. But another part of his personality bled at the sight of human suffering in East and West alike. It might appear that his mind seldom found a point of rest in its oscillation between thought of God and service to man. Be that as it may, he chose in obedience to a higher call, service to man as his mission on earth and this choice has endeared him to people in the west, Americans in particular. In the course of a short life of thirty-nine years (1863-1902), of which only ten years were devoted to public activities and those too in the midst of acute physical suffering, he left for descendents his four classics: *Jnana-Yoga*, *Bhakti-Yoga*, *Karma-Yoga*, and *Raja-Yoga*, all of which are outstanding discourses on Hindu philosophy. In addition, he delivered innumerable lectures, wrote inspired letters in his own hand to his many friends and disciples, composed numerous poems, and acted as spiritual guide to the many seekers who came to him for instruction. He also organized the Ramakrishna Order of monks, which is the most outstanding religious organization of modern India. It is devoted to the propagation of the Hindu spiritual culture not only in the Swami's native land, but also in America and in other parts of the world. Swami Vivekananda once spoke of himself as a 'condensed India.' His life and teachings are of inestimable value to the west for an understanding of the mind of Asia. William James, the Harvard philosopher, called the Swami the 'paragon of Vedantists.'[10] Max Muller and Paul Deussen, the famous Orientalists of the nineteenth century, admired him in genuine respect and affection.

Swami Vivekananda's inspiring personality was well known both in India and in America during the last decade of the nineteenth century and the first decade of the twentieth century. The unknown monk of India suddenly leapt into fame at the Parliament of Religions held in Chicago in 1893, at which he represented the soul ideals of Hinduism. His vast knowledge of Eastern and Western culture as well as his deep spiritual insight, ardent eloquence, brilliant conversation, broad human sympathy, colourful personality, and handsome figure made an irresistible appeal to the many types of Americans who came in contact with him. People who saw or heard Vivekananda even once still cherish his memory after a lapse of more than half a century. In America, Vivekananda's mission was the interpretation of India's spiritual culture, especially in its Vedantic setting. He also tried to enrich the religious consciousness of the Americans through the rational and humanistic teachings of the Vedanta philosophy. In America he became India's spiritual ambassador[11] and pleaded eloquently for better understanding between India and the New World in order to create a healthy synthesis of East and West, of religion and science. In his own motherland Vivekananda is regarded as the patriot-saint of modern India and an inspirer of her dormant national consciousness. To the Hindus he preached the ideal of a strength-giving and man-making religion. Service to man as the visible indication of the Godhead was the special form of worship he advocated for the Indians, devoted as they were to the rituals and myths of their ancient faith. Many political leaders of India have publicly acknowledged their indebtedness to Swami Vivekananda. He finally inspired that the Indian national life should be awakened and the vigorous Indians must conquest the world by 'Indian thought'. Indian thought means philosophical and spiritual, with its assistance once again go over and conquer the world. He instigated that, up India and conquer the world with your spirituality.

Patriotic views of Vivekananda

Subash Chandra Bose eulogized about Vivekananda, "He was so great, so profound, so talented. A yogi of the highest spiritual level in direct communion with the truth, who had, for the time being sacred his whole life to the moral and spiritual uplift of his nation and of humanity, that is how I would describe him. If he had been alive, I would have been at his feet. Modern India is his creation—if I err not".[12]

Swami Vivekananda's spiritual philosophy helped to raise the nationalist feelings among the young Indians. According to M.N. Roy, Vivekananda's spiritualism and nationalism both were inseparable because he was a hero-prophet and a patriot-saint of India. Mr M.N. Roy in 'India in Transition' wrote about Vivekananda—'His nationalism was spiritual imperialism'. He also informed that, Vivekananda called on young India to believe in the spiritual mission of India. His philosophy influenced greatly and subsequently built the orthodox nationalism of the declassed young intellectuals, organised into secret societies advocating violence and terrorism for the overthrow of British rule. Mr. Roy said that, he was a strong critic of social westernisation. Vivekananda wrote: "We must grow according to our nature; Vain is to attempt the lines of action that foreign societies have grafted upon us; it is impossible... Suppose you can imitate the westerners, that moment you will die, you will have no more life in you". He gave an inspiring call to Indians: "Thou brave one, be bold, take courage, be proud that thou art an Indian, and proudly proclaim. I am an Indian, every Indian is my brother." Mr. Roy applauded that, the teaching of Vivekananda had profound effect on the educated elite and the masses and facilitated[13] for the development of spirituality and national awakening. The great saint inspired the people of India to take action for the indictment of freedom.

Swami Vivekananda's patriotic quest was sent into the nerves of Indians and shook India from her slumber of unhappiness through his poetic expressions.[14] He directed that imitation is not civilisation. Do not behave like another race and think for genuine that it will be better for India; all the Indians should be dressed like Indians. He articulated regarding the weakness of Indians by saying that we have lost our faith. Why it is that we have been ruled by many foreign rulers for the last one thousand years and who chose to walk over prostrate bodies of ours. Because they have faith in themselves and we had not. Being a conquered race we have enhanced ourselves and believed that we are not weak and have to fight for our independence in anything. We have to develop faith in our own selves.[15]

Vivekananda had himself combined passionate evocation of the glories of the Aryan tradition and Hinduism with bitter attacks on present day degradation of 'Our religion is in the kitchen. Our God is the cooking pot.'[16] He preached this worldly type of religion, emphasizing self-help and the building-up of manly strength: 'What our country now wants are muscles of iron and nerves of steel.' Vivekananda's appeal, and his mixture of patriotism with the cult of manly virtues, vague populism, and evocation of Hindu glory was to prove stimulating wine indeed for young men in the coming of Swadeshi struggle.

Vivekananda advised that we cannot achieve without the associations of the world. We have many things to learn from west. We have to learn from the west her arts and sciences. We have to gain a little in material knowledge, in the power of organisation, in the ability to handle powers, organizing powers in bringing the best results in our routine life of small struggles. He also recommended that we must travel and go to foreign places. We must see how the engine of society works in other countries, and keep free and open communication with what is going on in the minds of other countries, if we really want to be a nation again. But remember that as Hindus everything else must be lower to our own national ideals. The secret of a true Hindu character lies in the subordination of his knowledge of

European science and learning, of his wealth, position and name, to that one principal theme which is inborn in every Hindu child—the spirituality and purity of the race. He questions that can you make a European society with Indian's religion? He replied that, it is possible and we must trust it.[17] The country has fallen, no doubt, but will sure rise again and the upheaval will surprise the world. If there is the darkness of centuries in a room and we go into the room and begin to cry. "Oh it is dark!" will the darkness go? Bring in the light and darkness will vanish at once.[18] Swami Vivekananda was favourably patriotic but there was no manner of difference in the national urge he tried to create and in the active internationalism in which he both strongly believed. Again he was successful in straining his utmost to stir up and bring to life the civic and social consciousness of the people of their times which had been covered with neglect and apathy.[19]

Views on Caste System

Vivekananda condemned the caste system and the Hindu emphasis on rituals and superstitions, and urged the people to imbibe the spirit of liberty, quality and free-thinking. Probably he never worked for the development of lower classes conditions in the society but he showed the sympathy in his speeches and appealed upper castes not to practise discrimination policy towards the downtrodden. Vivekananda believed that one of the causes of India's disgrace was the neglect of the low caste masses and that became the great national sin. The political principles or governments would not pay any attention for the low caste masses in India to ensure if they are well educated, well fed, and well cared for. He also said that, they pay for our education, they build our temples, but in return they obtained kicks. The masses that comprise the lowest caste, through ages of constant tyranny of the higher castes and by being treated with blows and jolts[20] at every step they took, have totally lost their manliness and become like professional beggars. Vivekananda advised to higher castes, if we want to regenerate India, we must work for them.

Equally remarkable was Vivekananda's concern for the plight of the 'Daridranarayana'. His famous appeal was that do not forget the lower classes, the ignorant, the poor, the illiterate, the cobbler, the sweeper, they are our flesh and blood, they are our brothers.[21] He therefore, advised the upper castes to dedicate themselves towards the service of 'Daridranarayana' (God manifested in the hungry, destitute millions) for their upliftment and edification.[22] Formerly the upper castes felt that only they were pure and the whole world was impure. They followed and assumed the principle of "Don't touch me!" "Don't touch me!" 'Now-a-day's Brahmins are neither in the recesses of the heart, nor in the highest heaven, nor in all beings now he is in the cooking pot!'

He said that, we are orthodox Hindus, but we refuse to touch others and entirely to identify ourselves as pure with "Don't-Touchism." That is not Hinduism; it is in none of our books; it is an orthodox superstition, which has hindered national efficiency and interest all along the line.[23] People were inclined to hold Hinduism, though all had equal rights to acquire tattva-jnana (knowledge of spirit), the difference of high and low should not be maintained in the day-to-day dealings and relations.[24] It was left to Swami Vivekananda to give this turn to the religious outlook of the Hindu by inculcating in him the ideal of self-dedication to the cause of the service of humanity, to awaken the downtrodden people, to rouse his countrymen to stand on their feet and to be men inspired with the spirit of Karma-yoga, which was his ideal. Swami Vivekananda developed and propagated the importance of Karmayoga, and, according to him, "action had to be accepted as all important and essential even in the man of religion".[25] This necessarily involved the fight against the ancient traditions according to which sanyasis of India had striven and struggled to realise their ideal of Mukthi, in isolation from society, and in meditation, thereby making them more or less lost to the outer world. This new approach of religious thought emphasised that the first and foremost duty of a man of religion in India was but boundless and unrelenting service rendered to his fellowmen without any distinction of religion, caste or creed.

Swami Vivekananda promulgated that according to Vedanta, one's duty was no more than putting one into the task of saving the fated ones. Thus, the ideal of a sanyasi in saffron garb was not only to dedicate his life for the spiritual upliftment but also to a drastic social reform and service to suffering humanity. He trusted on the Upanishads, which called leading the weak, the suffering and downtrodden, to stand on their feet and to be free from weakness.[26] Thus, mere worship of God with flowers and ritual yielded place to the worship of God by self-dedication and service to the cause of human beings who themselves belonged to and form of God. The universal soul and self-improvement sought by spiritual discipline was replaced by the effort of the self to serve the human cause, helping and uplifting the downtrodden. Thus service to man came to be regarded as service to God both being treated as one and the same.[27] He educated us, "The same soul resides in each and all. If you are convinced of this, it is your duty to treat all as brothers and serve mankind." [28]

Conclusion

Swami Vivekananda was the most influential person in Indian history. He was a revivalist and reformist, his thoughts relating to spirituality and humanity attracted both national and international arenas. The idea of the development of daridranaryana is completely attached to the Vedanta philosophy that recommends invaluable service to the low castes. His philosophy of oneness of religion or God has gained attention in western countries and has been prevalently propagated there by the Ramakrishna Mission. Even though he was a monk, his patriotic ideas greatly inspired the Indians. Especially the discourses of Vivekananda influenced many youngsters and they jumped into the Indian freedom movement. His nationalism and spiritualism both were inseparable. He said that we are all Indians but based on caste differences some of the low class masses were pushed far away from society and their services were not benefited to the country. Because of the caste differences, we lost our unity which is later benefited to invaders. So he advised the upper castes do not practise 'Don't Touch' policy which is not inscribed anywhere in Hindu texts. He suggested that Indians must go to foreign countries to learn their knowledge which helps us to avoid ignorance. He not only made us conscious of our strength, but also pointed out our defects and drawbacks. He made people conscious of the ignorance and unwisdom and the unity and fraternity.

REFERENCES

1. G.S.Banhatti, *Life and Philosophy of Swami Vivekananda*, Atlantic Publishers, 1995, p. 1.

2. Sen, Amiya, *Indispensible Vivekananda: anthology for our times*, Oriental Black Swan, New Delhi, 2006, p.11.

3. Sen, Amiya, Narayani Gupta, ed., *Swami Vivekananda*, Oxford Universiy Press, New Delhi, 2003, p. 19.

4. *Ibid.*, p. 20.

5. Chetananda Swami, *God Lived with them: life stories of sixteen monastic disciples of Sri Rama Krishna*, St. Louis, America, 1997, p.20.

6. Rolland, Romain, *The Life of Vivekananda and the Universal Gospel*, Advaita Ashram, Delhi, 2008, pp.16-18.

7. G.S.Chhabra, *Advanced Study in the History of Modern India, Vol-2 (1813-1920)* Lotus Press, New Delhi, 2005, p. 445.

8. Swami Vivekananda Birth centenary commemoration souvenir (1863- 1963), Madras, 1964, p.

9. Nikhilananda Swami, Swami Vivekananda - A Biography by Swami Nikhilananda, Ramakrishna-Vivekananda centre, New York, 1953, p.183

10. *Ibid.*, p.1

11. *Ibid.*, p.180

12. Swami Vivekananda Birth centenary commemoration souvenir (1863- 1963), Op. cit., p. 107

13. R.C.Agarwal, Constitutional Development and National Movement of India, part-I, S. Chand company, New Delhi, p. 91.

14. G.S.Chhabra, Advanced Study in the History of Modern India, Vol-2 (1813-1920) Lotus Press, New Delhi, 2005, p. 544.

15. Swami Vivekananda Birth centenary commemoration souvenir (1863-1963), Op. cit., p. 41.

16. Sumit Sarkar, Modern India 1885- 1947, Macmillan, Delhi,1983, pp.72,73.

17. Swami Vivekananda Birth centenary commemoration souvenir (1863-1963), Op. cit., pp. 41, 42.

18. *Ibid.*, p. 40.

101

19. *Ibid.*, p. 132.
20. *Ibid.*, pp.37, 38.
21. Sumit Sarkar ,Modern India 1885-1947, Op. cit., pp.72, 73.
22. Swami Vivekananda Birth centenary commemoration souvenir (1863-1963), Op. cit., P.132.
23. *Ibid.*, p.105.
24. *Ibid.*, p.132.
25. *Ibid.*, p.131.
26. *Ibid.*, p.130.
27. *Ibid.*, p.131.
28. *Ibid.*, p.132.

❧ Chapter 12 ❧

Swami Vivekananda's Progressive Thoughts

P. Charles Christopher Raj

Assistant Professor Of History
Kasthurba College For Women
Villianur, Puducherry 605 110

Introduction

Swami Vivekananda or Narendranath Datta, or simply Narendra or Naren as he was known during his pre-monastic days, was born to Vishwanath Datta and Bhuvaneshwari Devi on Monday, 12 January 1863 at Kolkata. He belonged to a high-caste, relatively affluent family of lawyers, and received a solid western style education. From the influence of his father, he seemed certain to enter into the profession of law. But, at the age of 18, he met Sri Ramakrishna, a revered Hindu ascetic who placed his hand on the young Anglophile and instantly tapped within him an undiscovered spring of traditional Hindu thought[1]. Vivekananda strove to rid Hindu society of the many ills that contaminated its pristine purity. His crusade against untouchability, his desire to uplift Indian women to the level of equality among men, and the new yet old orientation that he gave to education as 'the drawing yardstick of the perfection already in man', were part and parcel of his well-defined mission in life. His extraordinary gift of oratory struck his audiences like a lightning bolt and immediately propelled him into an unprecedented speaking tour throughout America and Europe.

His thoughts were dedicated to social service and religious education with centres around the globe, served the poor with great zeal, and proved contagious to the Indian Nationalist Movement, especially to Gandhiji's programme of social reform. His messages still remain clear and emphatic for the development of Indian women. Though he lived a life of celibacy, he talks in overwhelming terms about the greatness of love and marriage as well as the duties that are to be fulfilled by the householder[2].

His ideas bore the paradigm shift, and expected India to become a great power in 2020, a dream already visualized by Swamiji in the 19th century. In fact, he was the first entrepreneur behind the concept of globalization who took Hindu religion all over the world. He made aware that there is a religion which deals with progress in life that can be achieved with the help of a special instrument called 'Truth'. Swamiji's progressive thoughts were supererogatory, highly prominent and visible even in the present century.

Swamiji's views on Social evils and Remedies

On looking at the social evils of our country, he advocates the remedies through his teachings, that each soul is potentially Divine, the goal of human birth is to realize this Divinity within and manifest it for the welfare of the humanity, and essentially all religions lead to the same realization.

The important point to note is insistence on individual liberation as a priority over the efforts to 'do good to the world'. The idea is to strive for special state or plane of consciousness that would lead a person to realize his or her true nature. Achieving such exalted state of altered consciousness forms the basis for human actions. Every human act should have this aim in sight, and even in 'service to humanity and renunciation of sense pleasures'. Religion or spirituality was an act of inching higher and higher on the steps of consciousness, from animal consciousness to human consciousness, and from human consciousness to Divine Consciousness[3]. Remedies to the prevailing evil in the society is his summation through upward motion of faith in oneself, strength of the individual to face the society, fearlessness of any evil that engulfs the individual, truthfulness at all time of life and lastly service to humanity that alone can bring the ointment for the wound caused by the social evils of our country.

Swamiji and the Significance of Education

Swami Vivekananda, a great thinker embraces education and signifies it as a tool for 'man-making'. Realizing that mankind is passing through a crisis, he cautioned that our materialistic and mechanical way of life is fast reducing man to the status of a machine. He feels the dire need of awakening man to his spiritual self where in lies the very purpose of education.

Education is not mere literacy as he observes but it should be abound in information that can be disseminated, and should embody a culture. In his scheme of education, he lays great stress on physical health because a sound mind resides in a sound body and he quotes as 'nayamatma balahinema labhyah', i.e., the self cannot be realized by the philosophy of weak[4].

The exposition and analysis of Vivekananda's scheme of education brings to light its constructive, practical and comprehensive character. He realizes that is only through education that the upliftment of masses is possible.

A few of Swamiji's personal observations epitomize the concept of education that it acts as a tool of perfection found already in man. Like flintlocks, knowledge is well present in one's mind but suggestive ideas are the friction which brings it out. Education doesn't mean obeying Guru who taught you or blindly worshipping your Guru as God, love him as you will, but think for yourself[5].

He states it emphatically that if society is to be reformed, education has to reach everyone, high and low, because individuals are the very constituents of society. The sense of dignity rises in man when he becomes conscious of his inner spirit and that is the very purpose of education. He strives to harmonize the traditional values of India with the new values brought through the progress of science and technology.

It is in the transformation of man through moral and spiritual education that he finds the solution for all social evils. Founding education on the firm ground of our own philosophy and culture, he shows the best of remedies for today's social and global illness. Through his scheme of education, he tries to materialize the moral and spiritual welfare and upliftment of humanity, irrespective of caste, creed, nationality or time. However, Swami Vivekananda's scheme of education, through which he wanted to build up a strong nation that will lead the world towards peace and harmony, is still a far cry. It is high time that we give serious thought to his philosophy of education and remember his call to everybody–'Arise, awake, and stop not till the goal is reached.'

Swamiji on 'Women'—their Problems and Solutions

According to Swamiji, the Status of Women is that 'Women are bondage and a snare to men'. It is for this purpose, I suppose, that scriptural writers hint that knowledge and devotion are difficult of attainment to them? Swamiji replies, **"In what scriptures do you find statements that women are not competent for knowledge and devotion?"** In the period of degradation, when the priests made the other castes incompetent for the study of the Vedas, they deprived the women also of their rights. Otherwise you will find in the Vedic or Upanishad age Maitreyi, Gargi and other women of revered memory have taken the places of the Rishis through their skills in discussing the Brahman. All nations have achieved greatness by paying proper respect to women. **Manu says "Where women are respected, they are Gods delight, and where they are not, all works and efforts come to naught."** In India, **Women are revered as Mother**–The mother is the ideal of Indian womanhood.

And even God is conceived as mother. In the West, a woman is essentially a wife. In a western home it is the wife who rules but in an Indian home it is the mother who rules. Woman as mother is marvellous, unselfish and ever forgiving. In India it is the father who punishes the child, not the mother as in the West[6].

The most significant and profound solution to the existing problem is that all hearts should throng and start a movement for emancipation of women. Though the primary goal for women empowerment is to improve the quality of life of women but it has also deep ramifications in social, economic and political scenario of body polity. The media through its reach to people at large has been instrumental though not to the extent desired in supporting the movement for women emancipation by focusing neglect and marginalization of the position of the women in society. It sounds intriguing how from a highly dignified position in India's mythic history, the woman in India has been relegated to a secondary position. The vested interests of the ruling elite and the male lobby influenced by alien cultures legitimised woman as an individual of little consequence. It would be a sad commentary on the subordinate role of women in India when woman is ideally viewed as Shakti (Power), the origin of power itself but in reality found as helpless, hapless woman without any identity except that of a wife, or the mother who has very little voice in decision-making and has very little by way of her own basic choice. Although discrimination against and exploitation of women are global phenomena, their consequences are more tragic in some parts of the globe particularly in under-developed countries where, ignorance, deprivation of the basic necessities of life, and the ever-growing pressure of transition from tradition to modernity, all combine to aggravate the inequalities that women suffer to a point at which their existence is reduced to a continuous battle for survival. Improving the status of women is regarded as the key to narrowing the gender gap and achieving a better quality of life. Women are under great social control and scrutiny which has restricted what they can say, where and to whom. Cultural moves in almost every social set-up determine women's socialization in no uncertain terms. This has an important bearing on their ability to communicate and express their thoughts. Swamiji compared foreign women to Indian women, and stated that women should have the liberty; liberty as the first condition of growth, will help women in leading their own life independently, not depending on their husbands and sons at various stages of their life span[7].

He utters in his own lecture that 'Men and women in every country, have different ways of understanding and judging things. Men have one angle of vision, women another; men argue from one standpoint, women from another. Men extenuate women and lay the blame on men; while women exonerate men and heap all the heap on women'[8]. He entrusted the duty to incoming generation thinkers to uplift womanhood as scholars like Maitreyi and Gargi, heroines like the Queen of Jhansi; wives like Sita and mothers of heroes like Jeeja Bai[9].

Swamiji reminds us how in our old forest universities there was equality between boys and girls so that in this nation we may not have to learn from Tennyson's long poem *Princess* about educating a woman. Thus equality of sexes and freedom is the burden of Vivekananda's speeches and writings concerning women. But as Sister Nivedita points out, "The growth of freedom of which he dreamt, would be no fruit of agitation, clamorous and iconoclastic. It would be indirect, silent and organic[10]".

Swamiji on the "Institution of Marriage"

Swamiji utters that the most desirable life of a citizen in a society is the life of a family man with all the happiness that the company of a loving wife and loved children can offer. The life of the married man is quite as great as that of the celibate. It is useless to say that the man who lives out of the world is a greater man than he who lives in the world; it is much more difficult to live in the world and worship God than to give it up and live a free and easy life[11].

Marriage is the type of institution of one's soul in relation to God. He justified Hindu marriage customs, as springing from the pursuit of this ideal, and from the woman's need of protection, in combination. And he traced out the relation of the whole subject to the Philosophy of the Absolute. When Swamiji was with Sister Nivedita at Jhelum he discussed about the depth of marriage and said in his own words—"This is why"; he exclaimed, "though the love of a mother is in some ways greater, yet the whole world takes the love of man and woman as the type". No other has such tremendous idealizing power. The beloved actually becomes what he is imagined to be. This love transforms its object. Marriage is not for individual happiness, but for the welfare of the nation and the caste. Certain individuals of the modern reform, having embarked on an experiment which could not solve the problem, "are the sacrifices, over which the race has to walk"[12].

Swamiji's idea on Religion as the Healer of Humanity

Religion plays a vital role in the growth of a country. The world of religion has many prescriptions and many practices. The priestly order in every religion has its own dress and its own discipline. There are many rituals and many taboos. Individuals are expected to suffer penances, offer prayers, of a greater rigour and a life of asceticism all stipulated. Celibacy, renunciation and other practices are prescribed as paths to the heaven. Much has been said about the common ground of religious unity. This unity cannot come by the triumph of any one of the religions and by the destruction of others. It can come only by every religion assimilating the good points of other religions. To other nations, religion is one of the occupations of life but here in India, religion is the one and only occupation in life. As a consequence, our culture and national genius have derived a special bent or direction. Referring to the flooding of the world with Indian spiritual ideas that is silently taking place, German philosopher Schopenhauer said "The world is about to see a revolution in thought that is more extensive and more powerful than that was witnessed by the Renaissance of Greek literature.[13]" The Ideal of Universal Acceptance —What the world needs from India is the idea of harmony and acceptance of all religions. In the ancient world, outside India among the Babylonians and the Jews, each tribe had a God known as Baal and Moloch. When the tribes fought among themselves, the victor displaced the Baal or Moloch in the temple of the vanquished with its own God. Thus the supremacy of Gods was settled in battle. In India, religious evolution took a different turn. Here also there were several Gods, but it was realized in the Vedic times that Truth or God is one but the sages call him differently. Differentiation is the law of life and religious differences are bound to persist, but it does not mean that we should hate each other. This can be achieved only if the Truth of universal acceptance preached in India is spread the world over.

As Swami Vivekananda says in 'Is Vedanta The Future Religion?' "...Gradual or not gradual, easy or not easy for the weak, is not the dualistic method based on falsehood? Are not all the prevalent religious practices often weakening and therefore wrong? They are based on a wrong idea, a wrong view of man. Would two wrongs make one right? Would the lie become truth? Would darkness become light? ......Vedanta is everywhere; only you must become conscious of it. These masses of foolish beliefs and superstitions hinder us in our progress. If we can, let us throw them off and understand that God is spirit to be worshipped in Spirit and in Truth. ...All the different ideas of God, which are more or less materialistic, must go. As man becomes more and more spiritual, he has to throw off all these ideas and leave them behind. If Vedanta—this conscious knowledge that all is one Spirit—spreads, the whole humanity will become spiritual. But is it possible? I do not know...[14]"

Conclusion

It is well known that Swami Vivekananda was associated with the Renaissance in India, that he was one of the leading thinkers of the emerging new India at the turn of the 19th century. He was regarded as a prophet who gave a clarion call to a tired nation with a hoary culture to awake and arise. A whole culture was to be reborn from servitude, lassitude and fickleness. He could rejuvenate that culture, and act as its spiritual ambassador to the West. But it is perhaps not so well known that Swami Vivekananda was deeply committed to the welfare of women. One of the over-riding issues of the Indian Renaissance was the position of women in our society and the oppression women faced both at the institutional and individual levels. It is interesting to examine Swami Vivekananda's stand on the issue of women's rights. It reveals his deep insight into Indian culture and spiritual history, for they were responsible for shaping our tradition and traditional institutions. Vivekananda's call for the liberation of

India from its evils was very different from the shrill cry of the Western suffragette for franchise or "liberation". It is the result of an inclusive understanding of a whole way of life.

FOOTNOTES

1. Som Ranchan, *Swami Vivekananda Insan-E-Kamal*, Delhi, 1998, p.2-4.

2. P.Sankaranarayanan, *Our Motherland Swami Vivekananda*, Bombay, 1963, p.14.

3. *The Complete Works of Swami Vivekananda*, Calcultta, 1985, Volume VIII, p. 122.

4. T.S.Avinashilingam, *Education Compiled From The Speeches And Writings Of Swami Vivekananda*, Compiled And Edited By T.S.Avinashilingam, Coimbatore (Tamilnadu), India, 1943, p.3.

5. *The Complete Works of Swami Vivekananda*, Calcutta, 1985, Volume V, p 364.

6. *The Complete Works of Swami Vivekananda*, Calcutta, 1985, Volume VIII, p 252-253.

7. *The Complete Works of Swami Vivekananda*, Calcutta, 1985, Volume III, p 246.

8. *The Complete Works of Swami Vivekananda*, Calcutta, 1985, Volume VII, p 378.

9. V.C. Kulandaiswamy, *They thought Differently*, Tamilnadu, 1989, p.32.

10. Sister Nivedita, *The Master as I Saw him*, Calcutta 1983 p. 242.

11. *When Swami Vivekananda went to USA, a lady asked him to marry her. When Swami asked the lady about what made her ask him such question. The lady replied that she was fascinated by his intellect. She wanted a child of such an intellect. So she asked Swami, whether he could marry her and give a child like him. He said to that lady, that since she was attracted only by his intellect, there is no problem. "My dear lady, I understand Your desire. Marrying and bringing a child in to this world and understanding whether it is intelligent or not takes very long time. More over it is not guaranteed. Instead, to fulfill Your desire immediately, I can suggest a guaranteed way. Take me as Your*

child. You are my mother. Now on Your desire of having a child of my intellect is fulfilled." *The lady was speechless.*

http://wiki.answers.com/Q/Tell_me_something_about_swami_vive-kananda's_marriage.

12. *Notes of Some Wanderings With The Swami Vivekananda My Sister Nivedita of Ramkrishna-Vivekananda.* Edited By The Swami Saradan-anda, Calcutta, 1913, p 129.

13. V.C. Kulandaiswamy, *They thought Differently*, Tamilnadu, 1989, p. 32

14. *The Complete Works of Swami Vivekananda*, Calcutta, 1985, Volume VIII, p. 122.

Chapter 13

Swami Vivekananda's Ideals of Education

P. Sadish

Assistant Professor of History
Perunthalaivar Kamarajar Arts College,
Kalitheerthalkuppam,
Puducherry - 605 107.

Swami Vivekananda was one of the great educationalists of India and his contribution in the field of educational, spiritual, social and philosophical sphere was immemorial. He suggested the type of education that modern youth need today. According to Vivekananda, "Education is the manifestation of perfection already in man". Modern youth are facing enormous problems in the changing scenario of day-to-day life without adequate knowledge in education. Parents pressurise them to get good ranks, teachers expect the best performance and there are cut-throat competitions to secure jobs. Lack of proper understanding causes complex problems like depression, trauma, hatred, frustration, fear, disobedience, disorder of mind and sometimes even suicide.

On the other hand, electronic gadgets and media are contaminating their mind with vulgarity and obscenity because of which youth are lacking their moral character. His philosophy of education is man-making and character-building. Everything is lost when character is lost. The education our youth get today is just opposite to his idea of education.

According to Vivekananda, education remains incomplete without the teaching of aesthetics or fine arts. He points out that the combination of art and utility can make a nation great. The system of modern education and learning through book alone is not sufficient in solving the problems. His educational ideas are based on love, purity and equity combined with the whole world.

He was not in favour of bookish education. Vivekananda, in his scheme of education, meticulously included all aspects, which are necessary for all-around development of the body, mind and soul of the individual. Recognising his contribution, UNESCO has acknowledged Vivekananda as one of the eminent educationalist in the modern world.

This chapter is an attempt to explain the views of Swami Vivekananda and his ideals in the process of education.

What is Education?

Generally education is the delivery of knowledge, skills and information and values from teachers to students. Education plays a very significant role in curing the social evils, changing the destiny and shaping the future of humanity.

Education—What it Means According to Vivekananda?

It is not just reading a book. It is not trying to accumulate various skills. Education is to make our will power and habits channelize into a useful stream of purposeful power. Education is not the amount of information that is put into your brain and runs riot there, undigested, all your life.

True education is the one by which character is formed, strength of mind is increased, the intellect is expanded, and by which one can stand on one's own feet.[1] The training, by which the current and expression of will are brought under control and become fruitful, is called education.[2]

Vivekananda did not write any book on education but he contributed a lot of valuable thoughts on the subject matter of education. In order to understand his thoughts, we should first consider his definition of education—'Education is the manifestation of the perfection already in man.'[3]

The word 'manifestation' implies that something already exists and is waiting to be expressed. The main focus in learning is to make the hidden ability of a learner manifest. As Vivekananda said, 'what a man "learns" is really what he "discovers", by taking the cover off his own soul, which is a mine of infinite knowledge.'[4]

'Life-building, man-making, character-making assimilation of ideas' are the main ideals of education which will produce an integrated person—one who has learned how to improve his intellect, purify his emotions, and stand firm on moral virtues and unselfishness.

Real education is to enable one to stand on one's own legs. The education that you are receiving now in schools and colleges is only making you a race of dyspeptics. You are working like machines merely, and living a jelly-fish existence.[5]

The object of the ideal system of education should not merely be the advancement of theoretical knowledge but also the advancement of life, development of the highest powers and capacities, and the unfoldment of the noblest potentialities of the student. He must be enabled at the same time to apply intelligently to his own life all the ideas that he has learnt and gathered and thus promote his growth—physically, intellectually, morally and spiritually.

According to Swami Vivekananda there are several aims for education such as:

1. Self-Development
2. Fulfilment of Swadharma

3. Freedom of Growth

4. Character Formation

Self-Development

Vivekananda was contradicting the contemporary system of education. Vivekananda advocated education for self-development. According to the Indian philosophical tradition true knowledge does not come from outside, it is discovered within the self of individual, which is the source of all knowledge. According to Vivekananda, the function of education is the uncovering of the knowledge hidden in our mind.

Fulfilment of Swadharma

The idea of Swadharma in education is more significant according to Vivekananda. Everyone has to grow like himself. No one should copy others. External pressure only creates destructive reactions leading to stubbornness and disorderliness. In an atmosphere of freedom, love and sympathy alone, the child will develop courage and self-reliance. He should be taught to stand on his own, to be himself. Each child should be given opportunities to develop according to his own inner nature.

Freedom of Growth

Vivekananda is a staunch champion in education. Freedom is the first requirement for self-development. The child should be given freedom to grow according to his own nature. The teacher should not exert any type of pressure on the child. A teacher needs to help a student learn how to think, what to think, how to discriminate, how to appreciate things. The teacher should not possess knowledge to transmit to the student but also know how to transmit and the child should be helped in solving his problems himself. The teachers should have an attitude of service and worship. Education ultimately aims at realization. The only true teacher can immediately come down to the level of the student and transfer his soul to the soul of the student.[6]

Character Formation

"Neither money pays, nor name, not fame, nor learning, it is charac-ter that can cleave through adamantine walls of difficulties". - Swami Vivekananda.

Character is the foundation for self-development. The aim of education as self-development, therefore, leads to the aim of educa-tion for character. The aim of education is character-building. It de-pends upon the ideals cherished by the individual. The best way to develop a character is the personal example of high character set by the teacher. In the ancient system of Indian education, the teachers presented high ideals before the pupils and students imitated these ideals according to their capacities. Character-building was funda-mental in Vivekananda's educational scheme, as against career-ori-entation, which occupies centre-stage in today's education. A person is what his thoughts have made him. Explaining this, the Swami said, 'Each thought is a little hammer blow on the lump of iron which our bodies are, manufacturing out of it what we want it to be.'[7]

That is why one finds that the focus of the Swami's educational thoughts was on assimilation of man-making and character-build-ing ideas. Every thought and every move of a person leaves an im-pression on the mind. Character of a person is determined by some of the impressions. When large numbers of these impressions come together, they form habits. Through these acquisition and repetition of desirable habits, one's character can be remodelled. That is why Vivekananda said: "Words, even thoughts, contribute only one-third of the influence in making an impression; the man, two-thirds." [8] Therefore he desired that the teacher's life and personality should be like a blazing fire which could have a positive influence on the pupils in his care. Exposure to exemplary role models, particularly when they are teachers, and also to wholesome curriculum materials that impart culturally approved values to the young, is critical to charac-ter education.

Character-building education might focus on what is right and wrong teaching. But simultaneously, or alternatively, it should teach how to decide what is right and wrong. The present education system has overemphasised the cultivation of the intellect at cost of the general well-being of humanity. To check this dangerous trend, Vivekananda strongly recommended all round development of human beings. He expressed his desire in one of his lecture that 'all men were so constituted that in their minds of all these elements of philosophy, mysticism, emotion, and of work were equally present in full, that is ideal, my ideal of a perfect man.'[9] Vivekananda expected that the education systems would be suitably designed to produce such wholesome human beings. Interestingly the UNESCO report on learning to be published in 1972 while defining the aims of education echoed this same idea, accordingly, "the physical, the intellectual, emotional, and ethical integration of the individual into a complete man is a broad definition of the fundamental aim of education."[10]

Why religion forms the very foundation of education is clear in his following words: 'In building up character, in making for everything that is good and great, in bringing peace to others, and peace to one's own self, religion is the highest motive power, and, therefore, ought to be studied from that standpoint'. He believes that if education with its religious core can invigorate man's faith in his divine nature and the infinite potentialities of the human soul, it is sure to help man become strong, yet tolerant and sympathetic. It will also help man to extend his love and goodwill beyond the communal, national and racial barriers.

The following essential features are required for character formation:

Hard Work Character formation, according to Vivekananda, requires hard work. This is not possible by those who have a wish for all types of enjoyment. The best teacher for char acter-building is struggle. Dreams can never become a reality without hard work. Nothing can be great unless we work hard.

Moral and Spiritual Values Besides hard work, character formation requires traits such as purity, thirst for knowledge, perseverance, faith, humanity, submission and veneration, etc. These qualities may be developed by the teacher's example and the pupil's efforts.

Gurukula System   Relationship between the teacher and the taught is possible only in a Gurukula system of education. Therefore, Vivekananda favoured the ancient Indian Gurukula system of education. In these Gurukulas, the pupils served the teacher, who in his turn helped the pupils everywhere to achieve knowledge.

Formation of Good Habits   Character is intimately connected with habits. Habits express character. Good habits make for good character.

Learning through Mistakes   The child should be allowed to commit mistakes in the process of character formation. He will learn much by his mistakes. Errors are the stepping stones to our progress in character. Strong will, is the sign of great character.

Will makes Man Great   Vivekananda himself was an ideal teacher. His words worked like magic upon men and women. Vivekananda asked the people to build up their character and manifest their real nature which is 'the Effulgent, the Resplendent and the Ever Pure'.

According to Swami Vivekananda, the basic purpose of education is the total development of human personality. Everyone is endowed with certain capacities, which remain dormant, although in a potential form, in childhood. Swami Vivekananda believed education is the process by which these inherent potentialities in human personality manifest themselves in completing his or her total development.

Teacher and Student Relationship

Swami Vivekananda gives dignified place to the teacher. Teacher plays significant role in the formal process of education. Without teacher the process of education is ineffective. Proper education is possible through the interaction between the teacher and the taught. Teacher is the real textbook for his pupil. He trains the students' minds, cultivates their manners and shapes the morals of the members of the community at their most impressionable age. Teacher is the second parent of the student because parents give them life but teacher teaches them the art of living well. Teacher is the source of creativity to the students. Teacher in the name of Guru removes the darkness of ignorance.

Education and Poor Masses

Vivekananda was the first Indian leader who sought solution for the problem of the poor masses through education. He emphasised that unless there was uniform circulation of national blood all over the body, the nation could not rise. It was the duty of the upper classes, who had received their education at the expense of the poor, to come forward and uplift the poor through education. As he said once, "there must be equal chance to all, or if greater for some and for some less, the weaker should be given more chance than the strong."[11]

They are often victims of malnutrition, poor hygienic conditions and overcrowded housing. For the sustainable regeneration of India, most important priority must be given to educating the masses and restoring their individuality. They should not only be given education but also ideas, moral training and an understanding of their own historical situation for the self-reliance and work out for their salvation.

"The only service to be done for our lower classes is to give them education to develop their lost individuality. They are to be given ideas; their eyes are to be opened to what is going on in the world around them; and then they will work out their own salvation. Every nation, every man, and every woman must work out their own salvation. Give them ideas—that is the only help they require and then the rest must follow as the effect. Ours is to put the chemicals together, the crystallization comes in the law of nature".[12]

Educating the Women

He was very clear in the process of women's education; he stressed that women should be educated and it is the women who mould the next generation. Upliftment of women was the highest priority in the educational ideas of Vivekananda. According to him, "they (women) have many and grave problems, but none that are not to be solved by that magic world 'education.'"[13]

'Educate your women first and leave them to themselves; then they will tell you what reforms are necessary for them.'[14]

"I ask you all so earnestly to do likewise and open girls' schools in every village and try to uplift them. If the women are raised, then their children will by their noble actions glorify the name of the country—then will culture, knowledge, power, and devotion awaken in the land."[15] He realizes that if women of our country get the right type of education, then they will be able to solve their own problems in their own way. The main objective of his scheme of female education is to make them strong, fearless and conscious of their chastity and dignity. According to him, men and women are equally competent in academic matters, yet women have a special aptitude and competence for studies relating to home and family. Therefore he recommends the introduction of subjects like sewing, nursing, domestic science, culinary art, etc., which were not the part of education during his time.

Technical Education

Swami Vivekananda was one of the first among religious teachers to give importance to science and technology. At first Vivekananda saw that poor countries like India would be able to overcome poverty, starvation and backwardness only by mastering technology. Secondly, he saw that science is not contradictory to the eternal spiritual principles, which is the foundation of Indian culture. Both science and eternal religion are concerned with truth. Science seeks truth in the physical world, whereas religion seeks truth in the spiritual realm. Thus, both religion and science are complementary.

It is a misinterpretation of Vivekananda's philosophy of education to think that he has overemphasised the role of spiritual development to the utter neglect of the material side. Vivekananda, in his plan for the regeneration of India, repeatedly presses the need for the eradication of poverty, unemployment and ignorance. He says, we need technical education and all else which may develop industries, so that men, instead of seeking for service, may earn enough to provide for themselves, and save something against a rainy day. He feels it necessary that India should take from the Western nations all that are good in their civilization. However, just like a person, every nation has its individuality, which should not be destroyed. The individuality of India lies in her spiritual culture. Hence in Vivekananda's view, for the development of a balanced nation, we have to combine the dynamism and scientific attitude of the West with the spirituality of our country. The entire educational program should be so planned that it equips the youth to contribute to the material progress of the country as well as to maintaining the supreme worth of India's spiritual heritage. His popular saying proves the fact as follows:

"If I can get some unmarried graduates, I may try to send them over to Japan and make arrangements for their technical education there, so that when they come back, they may turn their knowledge to the best account for India. What a good thing that would be."[16]

"It would be better if the people got a little technical education, so that they might find work and earn their bread, instead of dawdling about and crying for service."[17]

Conclusion

The exposition and analysis of Vivekananda's scheme of education brings to light its constructive, practical and comprehensive character. Through his scheme of education, he tries to materialize the moral and spiritual welfare and upliftment of humanity, irrespective of caste, creed, nationality or time. However, implementing of Swami Vivekananda's scheme of education, through which he wanted to build up a strong nation that will lead the world towards peace and harmony, still remains a far cry. It is high time that we give serious thought to his philosophy of education and remember his call to everybody—'Arise, awake, and stop not till the goal is reached.'

'Traveling through many cities of Europe and observing in them the comforts and education of even the poor people, brought to my mind the state of our own poor people and I used to shed tears. What made the difference? "Education" was the answer I got.' He strives to harmonize the traditional values of India with the new values brought through the progress of science and technology. Education has to reach everyone, high and low, because individuals are the very constituents of society. The sense of dignity rises in man when he becomes conscious of his inner spirit, and that is the very purpose of education. "Help and not fight, assimilation and not destruction, harmony and peace and not dissention" was his motto and he rendered valuable service to the upliftment of mankind.

NOTES AND REFERENCES

1. Complete Works of Swami Vivekananda. Vol. V, p. 342. (Hereafter CW)
2. CW, Vol. IV, p.490.
3. CW, Vol. IV, p. 358.
4. CW, Vol. I, p. 28.
5. CW, Vol. VII, pp.147-8
6. CW, Vol. III, p. 183.
7. CW, Vol. VII, p. 20.
8. CW, Vol. II, p. 14.
9. CW, Vol. II, p. 388.
10. Edgar Faure et al., *Learning to be,* Paris: UNESCO, 1972, p.156.
11. CW, Vol. VI, p. 319.
12. CW, Vol. IV, p. 362.
13. CW, Vol. V, p. 231.
14. CW, Vol.VI, p.115.
15. CW, Vol. VII, p. 220.
16. CW, Vol. V, p. 372.
17. CW, Vol. V, p. 367.

WORKS ABOUT SWAMI VIVEKANANDA

.   Ahluwalia, B. *Vivekananda and the Indian Renaissance.* New Delhi: Associated Publishing Co.1983.

.   Avinashalingam T.S. *Educational philosophy of Swami Vivekananda.* 3rd ed. Coimbatore.1974. Sri Ramakrishna Mission Vidyalaya.

- Swami Vivekananda. (compiled by Kiran walia) *My ideal of education*, Advaita Ashrama, Kolkatta.2008.

- Swami Vivekananda. *Education.* Sri Ramakrishna Math Madras, 1998.

- Swami Bodhasarananda, *Selections from the complete works of Swami Vivekananda.* Advaita Ashram, Kolkata, 2007.

- Swami Srikandananda, *Youth! Arise Awake and Know Your Strength*, Vivekananda Institute of Human Excellence. Hyderabad. 2008.

- Santosh Kuma Behera, Educational *Ideas of Swami Vivekananda: perception of the essential nature of a teacher, the taught, methods of teaching and the discipline.* Samwaad: e - journal. Vol. 1. No. 1. 2012.

❧ Chapter 14 ❧

The End of all Education is Man-Making

S. Suriyakumari

Trained Graduate Teacher
Veeramamunivar Boys High school
Puducherry

India had not only always been the destination of learning and pioneer in principles of teaching in the historic past, but also has its credit on the philosophy of education and all related aspects like knowledge, intelligence, mind and the functions of teaching and learning from Vedic resources. Our land is proud to solicit a vast list of illustrious teachers of yore like Sri Krishna, Vidura, Bhisma, Dronacharya, Kribacharya from the Mahabharata and Vashista in the Ramayana followed by teachers like Susruta, Buddha and Mahavira. Textual evidences of their principles of teaching and learning embodied in their teachings. The quality of Indian discourse on Teaching and Learning has been widely acknowledged. There are many more examples during the medieval times of effective teachers, both of the religious and vocational kinds, which may be taken as the main foundations of educational thoughts of the present times.

In the modern India too there have been many original think-ers on education, say Vivekananda, Tagore, Aurobindo, Tilak, Zakir Husain, Radhakrishnan and above all, Mahatma Gandhi.

Meaning of Education from the Point of View of Indian Thinkers [1]

(i)   Makes man self-reliant and selfless. - Rigveda

(ii)   End-product, salvation. - Upanishads

(iii)   Makes man a good product. - Yajnavalkya

(iv)   Training for the country. - Kautilya

(v)   The realization of the self - Shankracharya

(vi)   Manifestation of the Divine perfection. - Vivekananda

(vii)   Means for character formation. - Dayananda

(viii) All-round drawing out of the best in body, mind, spirit. - Gandhi

(ix)   Makes life in harmony with all existence. - Tagore

(x)   Helping the growing soul to draw out that is in itself. - Aurobindo

(xi)   Dynamic process. - Humanyun Kabir

(xii)   Process getting to its full possible development. - Zakir Hussain

Education under British Raj brought a new system of western world oriented education, that led to a search for a better system of education in the country among the reformers and intellectuals. With time, a good deal of thinking, combined with actual experi-mentation on various alternative models of education had taken place. Present educational transitions are reflecting their decisions and genuinely attempts to bring in their contributions within the mainstream of the process of teaching and learning. At this juncture, I would like to quote the emphatic lines of Valentine Chirol who in his book *Indian Unrest* (1910)[2] stated:

The fundamental weakness of our Indian educational system is that the average Indian student cannot bring his education into any direct relation with the world in which, outside the class or lecture room, he continues to live. For that world is still the old Indian world of his forefathers, and it is as far removed as the poles as under from the Western world which claims his education.

The present situation is no better, even after a century of advanced system of education. Almost during the same time, Vivekananda illustrated the world that there is a close connection between culture and education. Wherever there is a great culture, we will find behind it, a highly developed system of education. Ancient India could produce a great culture because it developed a wonderful system of education. In those days, people took education seriously. As per the Taittiriya Upanishad, true tapas is—"study and teaching alone". Education itself is the best tapas, that is, the best form of human effort [3.]

Like all other great thinkers, Swami Vivekananda also accorded that the basic purpose of education is the total development of human personality. As per his idea, everyone is endowed with certain capacities, which remain dormant, although in a potential form, in childhood. Swami Vivekananda believed the process of education should bring out and manifest these inherent potentialities of human personality to help to attain the intellectual and moral development [4].

According to Vivekananda, the ultimate aim of true education is towards:

The Goal of Man-making

The end of all education, all training, should be man-making. The end and aim of all training is to make the man grow. The training by which the current and expression of will are brought under control and become fruitful, is called education. What our country now wants are

muscles of iron and nerves of steel, gigantic wills which nothing can resist, which can penetrate into the mysteries and secrets of the universe and will accomplish their purpose in any fashion, even if it means going down to the bottom of the ocean, meeting death face to face.

It is man-making religion that we want

It is man-making theories that we want.

It is man-making education all-round that we want.

Swami Vivekananda

According to Swamiji all material and spiritual knowledge is already present in man covered by a curtain of ignorance. Education should tear off that veil so that the knowledge shines forth as an illuminating torch to enliven all the corners. This is meant by achieving fullness of the latent perfection. In order to achieve this education which leads to real perfection, he has presented well conceived views that are applicable to all seasons of learning.

Attain Physical and Mental Development

Child of today, must be enabled to promote national growth and advancement as a fearless and physically well developed citizen of tomorrow. Stressing the mental development of the child, Swamiji, wished education to enable the child to stand on his own legs economically rather than becoming a parasite on others.

Achieve Moral and Spiritual Development

A nation's greatness is measured by the greatness of its citizens. But the greatness of citizens is possible only through their moral and spiritual development which education should foster.

Enhance one's Personality/Character

Character development is a very important aim of any education. For this, he emphasized the practice of Brahmacharya which fosters development of mental, moral and spiritual powers leading to purity of thoughts, words and deeds.

Progress in Faith on Oneself and Renunciation

Swamiji exhorted the individuals to keep full confidence upon their powers. They should inculcate a spirit of self-surrender, sacrifice and renunciation of material pleasures for the good of others. Education should inculcate all these qualities in the individual. He gave this call to his countrymen—"Arise, awake and stop not till the goal is achieved."

Role of a Child in the Arena of Education

Vivekananda emphasized the child-centred education. According to him, the child is already endowed with all learning, spiritual experience. Like a plant, a child grows by his own inner power naturally. Hence he advises the child to grow naturally and spontaneously, "Go into your own and get the Upanishads out of your own self. You are the greatest book that ever was or will be. Until the inner teacher opens, all outside teaching is in vain."[5]

Responsibilities of a Teacher

As nature to Wordsworth, it is a teacher to Vivekananda, who is to serve as a friend, philosopher and guide to a learner. He had complete faith on self-education. And insisted each one to be his/her own teacher. The external teacher only guides and inspires the inner teacher (soul) to rise up and start working to develop the child.

Method of Education

Vivekananda's method of education resembles the heuristic method of the modern educationists. In this system, the teacher invokes the spirit of inquiry in the pupil who is supposed to find out things for himself under the bias-free guidance of the teacher.

Swamiji lays a lot of emphasis on the environment at home and school for the proper growth of the child. The parents and teachers should inspire the child by their way of living. Swamiji recommends the old institution of Gurukula (living with the preceptor) and similar systems for the purpose. In such systems, the students develop an ideal character with the teacher constantly before them as the role model to follow. Though Swamiji stress mother tongue as the right medium for social or mass education, he prescribes the learning of English and Sanskrit also. While English is necessary for mastering western science and technology, Sanskrit leads one into the depths of our vast store of classics. Education, according to Swamiji, remains incomplete without the teaching of aesthetics or fine arts. He cites Japan as an example of how the combination of art and utility can make a nation great [6].

Ideas on Mass Education

"If the poor cannot come to education, education must reach them at the plough, in the factory, everywhere. Let unselfish, good and educated men go from village to village bringing not only religion to the door of everyone but also education"[7], said Swami Vivekananda. An ideal society, according to Vivekananda, should provide the resources as well as the opportunity for each of its members to develop his or her potential to the maximum. The education that does not help the common mass of people to equip themselves for the struggle for life, which does not bring out strength of character, as spirit of philanthropy and the courage of a lion, is it worth the name? Despite of the present shift of education from family, missionaries to sate the dream is yet to be achieved completely. The right to education for everyone, guaranteed by the Constitution of India, has brought a concrete form to the vision of Swamiji. Thanks to the present concerns of UNESCO[8] which has remarkable similarities to the thoughts of Vivekanada:

- His commitment towards universal values and tolerance, his active identification with humanity as a whole.

- The struggle in favor of the poor and destitute, to reduce poverty and to eliminate discrimination against women—reaching the unreached.

- His vision of education, science and culture as the essential instruments of human development.

- That education should be a lifelong process.

- And the need to move away from rote learning.

The lack of basic necessities among the underprivileged all over the world is no less striking than the lack of morality among the educated privileged ones. To squarely meet this great challenge, Vivekananda prescribed 'man-making and character-building education'[9].

Education for women

Another important aspect of Swamiji's scheme of education is women's education. He realizes that if the women of our country get the right type of education, then they will be able to solve their own problems in their own way. The main objective of his scheme of female education is to make them strong, fearless, and conscious of their chastity and dignity. He observes that although men and women are equally competent in academic matters, yet women have a special aptitude and competence for studies relating to home and family. Hence he recommends the introduction of subjects like sewing, nursing, domestic science, culinary art, etc., which were not parts of education at his time. The government of India has already implemented the right to education bill [10], with this the reach of education to girls becomes compulsory.

In addition to the above said features he emphasizes on:

Free Growth

In everyone there are infinite tendencies which require proper scope for satisfaction. Violent attempts at reform always end by retarding reform. If you do not allow one to become a lion, one will become a fox.

Positive Ideas

Positive ideas should only be given. Negative thoughts weaken men. The teaching must be modified according to the needs of the taught. Past lives have moulded our tendencies, and so give to the pupil according to his tendencies. Take everyone where he stands and push him forward. Sri Ramakrishna always gave words of hope and encouragement even to the most degraded of persons and lifted them up.

Liberty is the first condition of growth. As teachers one can only serve. Serve the children of the Lord if they have the privilege. If the Lord grants that they can help anyone of His children, blessed they are. Blessed they are that privilege was given to them when others had it not. So teaching should be done only as worship.

Assimilation of Ideas

Education is not the amount of information that is put into one's brain and runs riot there. Instead life-building, man-making, character-making, and assimilation of ideas are important. If these ideas are assimilated and made into life and character, one is more educated than any man who has got by heart a whole library. If education were identical with information, the libraries would be the greatest sages in the world and encyclopaedias, the Rishis.

The education that does not help the common mass of people to equip themselves for the struggle for life, which does not bring out strength of character, a spirit of philanthropy and the courage of a lion has no worth in itself.

Concentration: The Only Method of Education

There is only one method by which to attain knowledge, that which is called concentration. The very essence of education is concentration of mind. From the lowest man to the highest yogi, all have to use the same method to attain knowledge. The more the power of concentration is, greater the knowledge that is acquired.

The power of concentration is the only key to the treasure-house of knowledge. To him, the very essence of education is concentration of mind, not the collection of facts.

Brahmacharya

Power comes to him who observes unbroken Brahmacharya for a period of twelve years. Complete continence gives great intellectual and spiritual power. Controlled desire leads to the highest results. By observance of strict Brahmacharya, all learning can be mastered in a very short time: one acquires an unfailing memory of what one hears or knows but once. The chaste brain has tremendous energy and gigantic will power. Without chastity there can be no spiritual strength. Unchaste imagination is as bad as unchaste action. The Brahmacharin must be pure in thought, word and deed.

Where we went Wrong?

Most of the present day school and college curriculum only aim at intellectual development. It is in this field that western science, technology and commerce have attained tremendous success. Science is systematic pursuit of knowledge at empirical level. The scientific method gives a very good training to the mind. No one could deny that it was by applying the scientific method, western countries made tremendous advancement in technology and acquired great wealth and power. Swami Vivekananda was one of the first among religious teachers to understand the importance of science and technology. Swamiji always emphasized poor countries like India would be able to overcome poverty and backwardness only by mastering technology. Moreover Swamiji saw that science is not contradictory to the eternal spiritual principles, which is the foundation of Indian culture. Both science and eternal religion are concerned with truth. Science seeks truth in the physical world, whereas religion seeks truth in the spiritual realm. Thus, religion and science are complementary [11]. The other primary purpose of education is to build character and to enable people to lead moral lives. However, this is precisely the field where most of the modern systems of education have failed. Swami Vivekananda has given a new definition of morality. To quote his words, "The only definition that can be given of morality is this: that which is selfish is immoral, and that which is unselfish is moral"[12]; to him unselfishness and service are not mere matters of rules and regulations but of reality.

Conclusion

Vivekananda realized that mankind was passing through a crisis. The tremendous emphasis on the scientific and mechanical ways of life was reducing man to the status of a machine. Undermined moral and religious values and ignored principles of civilization led men to inner conflicts of ideals, manners and habits. To Vivekananda the solutions to all these social and global evils lie in the very purpose of education. Interestingly, Swami Vivekananda had envisioned a society with a new type of human being in whom knowledge, action, work and concentration were harmoniously blended, and he proposed a new type of education for achieving this. Swami Vivekananda's ideas on education still remain relevant and we have to keep ourselves motivated until the goal of universal education is achieved.[13] Astonishingly by the name of *Universalisation of Education,* with the support of UNESCO[14] the latest national curriculum Framework 2005[15] of our country recommends integrated learning that associates classroom learning with the society at every sphere. In addition, his thoughts on teaching are well beyond the contemporary standards in schools. The use of visual methods and story telling approaches[16] in teaching are now well recognized as efficient methods.

EXTERNAL REFERENCES, LINKS AND WORKS CITED

1. V.R. Taneja, V.R. Taneja & S. Taneja,
    Educational Thinkers
    Publisher Atlantic Publishers & Dist, 2006
2. Archival material relating to Ignatius Valentine Chirol
3. Education System In Ancient India.
4. Vivekananda's thoughts on education , Padakshep Blog
5. &12. Inspiring Thoughts of Swami Vivekananda On Education And Society Part 1 by Viswanadham Vangapally on *Apr 16, 2009*
6. Education In The Vision Of Swami Vivekananda By Dr. Sudipa Dutta Roy, July 2001
7. Advaita Ashrama (1983), *Reminiscences of Swami Vivekananda* (3 ed.), Calcutta, India: Advaita Ashrama, p. 430, ISBN 81-85301-17-4 (Collected articles on Swami Vivekananda, reprinted in 1994). Courtesy and Copyright Prabuddha Bharata.
8. &14. http://www.unicef.org/wcaro/4501_5112.html
9. (i) Swami Vivekananda Foundation,
    (ii) What is the Meaning of Education in Indian and Western Context?
    Senthil Kumar
    Education
10. 15&16. http://education.nic.in/Elementary/elementary.asp
11. Letter to Shrimati Sarala Ghosal,
    http://www.ramakrishnavivekananda.info/vivekananda/complete_works.htm
13. (i) http://www.un.org/millenniumgoals/education.shtml
    (ii) http://www.littlemag.com/hunger/aks.html
    (iii) http://www.ramakrishnavivekananda.info/vivekananda/complete_works.htm

Chapter 15

Swami Vivekananda's View on Emancipation of Women

M. Raji

Trained Graduate Teacher
Thiruvalluvar GGHSS
Department of Education
Puducherry.

"You can tell the status of a nation by looking at the status of its women"

-India's first Prime Minister Jawaharlal Nehru

Indian society is still largely male-dominated, and most women do not have real freedom. A cultural struggle is needed to sweep away the feudal and medieval mentality from which such a situation stems. The following is an attempt to analyze and examine the concept of their regeneration, and an argument for gender equality. Among the modern Indian reformers and leaders, who stood completely for women's equality and education was Swami Vivekananda. **Swami Vivekananda** (birth name Narendranath Datta, 1863-1902), **the most inspiring personalities of India** of late 19th century, did a lot to make India a better place to live in, and is known globally for his enchanting vision, spiritual wisdom and gender concern. Within **a short span of time, he** worked effortlessly to try and uplift the plight of women, in particular Indian women.

View on Soul

Swami Vivekananda was not only a visionary, or monk but a nationalist and a reformer par excellence. He at one time saw women as an obstacle. However on realising the highest truth he saw no distinction between sex and saw in women the presence of the Divine Mother. "The soul has neither sex, nor caste nor imperfection, it is neither male nor female, as there is no any sex distinction in *atman* (soul)". He argued that "It is very difficult to understand why in India, so much difference is made between men and women, whereas the Vedanta declares that one and the same conscious Self is present in all beings".

He criticized men, that they have turned the women into manufacturing machines. "If you do not raise the women, who are living embodiment of the Divine Mother, don't think that you have any other way to rise. Where women are respected, there the gods delight; and where they are not, there is no hope of rise for that family or country where they live in sadness" (CWV*, V, 7:214-15). Swami Vivekananda felt, the best thermometer to the progress of a nation is the treatment of its women and it is impossible to get back India's lost pride and honor unless they try to better the condition of women. He considered men and women as two wings of a bird, and it is not possible for a bird to fly on only one wing.

He said almost everywhere women are treated as playthings. Eknath Ranade warned that until the women learn to ignore the question of sex and to meet on a ground of common humanity they will not really develop and remain merely as playthings in the hands of men (Ranade, 1963: 108).

Vedic Period

Vivekananda studied about the history of the Indian women and the Vedic concept of women of the Aryan race. According to the Aryan, "a man cannot perform a religious action without his wife" (CWV*, 1997. V, 5:229). In that race, men and women were priests, "sapatimini (saha-dharmini)" or co-religionists as the Vedas call them... There man and wife together offered their sacrifices for that reason no unmarried man could become a priest. In the Vedic and Upanishadic age, Maitreyi, Gargi and other ladies of revered memory had taken the places of Rishis through their skill in discussing about Brahman. When such women were entitled to spiritual knowledge, Swamiji asks, then why shall not the women have the same privilege now? "It was a female sage who first found the unity of GOD (Generating, Ordaining, Destroying), and laid down this doctrine in one of the first hymns of the Vedas (CWV*, V, 4:170). Therefore, if even one amongst the women became a knower of Brahman, then by the radiance of her personality thousands of women would be inspired and awakened to truth, and great well-being of the country and society would ensure"(CWV*, V, 7:215-19).

View on Motherhood

"Woman has suffered for aeons and that has given her infinite patience and infinite perseverance". According to Vivekananda, the ideal of womanhood in India is motherhood— "In India the mother is the center of the family and a representative of God. Mother represents colourless love that knows no barter, unselfish and all forgiving love that never dies. Who can have such love?—only mother, not son, nor daughter, nor wife" (CWV*, V, 6:149). He saw their love as eternal. He said, "Mother is the first manifestation of power and is considered a higher idea than father". "Motherhood is the beginning. Motherhood is the end of Indian womanhood" (Maithilyananda, 1959). To him women were living images of Shakti--the Divine Mother.

Understanding Capacity

Men and women in every country, have different ways of understanding and judging things. Men extenuate women and lay the blame on men; while women exonerate men and heap all the heap on women (CWV*, V, 7:378). We are not men and women, but only human beings, born to cherish and to help one another. He said "Liberty of thought and action is the only condition of life, of growth and well-being. Where it does not exist, the race, the nation must go". The whole universe is one of perfect balance (CWV*, V, 2:25-26). Here interdependence is the law; it alone leads to happiness and fulfillment for both. To elaborate this in the words of Gandhi, "woman has as much right to shape her own destiny as man has to shape his and rules of social conduct must be framed by mutual co-operation and consultation" (Sharma, 1981: 49). In his opinion, divorces do not occur in India in many cases because, "the strongest love in the world is that between man and woman, and that also when it is clandestine" (CWV*, V, 6:115). That is, love should not be for fulfillment of lust only.

Men and women are complementary to each other and wonderful as they are, but by this I don't mean that women can't do something which men can. God made women endowed with tremendous mental strength through which she can achieve anything, gifted with motherly affection, softness and made her immensely possessive about her family. Swami Vivekananda aptly said, women are not useless but are used less. "If you do not allow women to become a lion, she will become a fox. Women are a power, only now it is more evil because man oppresses woman; she is the fox, but when she is no longer oppressed, she will be the lion" (CWV*, V, 5:22). With five hundred men, the conquest of India might take fifty years; with as many women not more than a few weeks.

American Women

Swami Vivekananda noticed in modern countries like America, women have more independence, he adds that men bow low, offer a woman a chair. After travelling through America, he mentioned "Nowhere in the world are women like those of this country.

How pure, independent, self-relying and kind hearted! It is the women who are the life and soul of the country. All learned and culture centered in this country. There are thousands of women here whose minds are as pure and as white as snow of this country". Then he said about the Indian women, "becoming mothers below their teens! I now see it all". He understood the paradox of Manu's dictum, "The Gods are pleased when the women are held high in esteem" but the reality of women's position makes us horrible sinners, and our degradation is due to our calling women 'despicable worms', 'gateways to hell' and so forth. (CWV*, V, 6:252-553).

Education

The idea of perfect womanhood is perfect independence. Swamiji found the magic word "education" as the best and only device to solve all problems of women and thereby emancipate them (CWV*, V, 3:302). "Education which does not bring out the strength of character, a spirit of philanthropy and the courage of a lion is not worth being called education". His method of solving things was "to take out by the roots the very causes of the disease and not to keep them merely suppressed" (CWV*, V, 5:334). For Vivekananda women are but a part of divinity; why should they be afraid of anything? He constantly said "Be fearless and be strong. If there is a sin in the world it is weakness; avoid all weakness, weakness is death". Fear breeds evil and weeping and wailing. Anything that makes you weak physically, intellectually and spiritually, reject as poison, there is no life in it, it cannot be true.

Self-Confidence and Perseverance

A precursor to do anything in life is to have confidence in the self. He attached more importance to self-confidence than even faith in God! For any endeavor to attain the pinnacle of success, dedication to the cause is absolutely essential. He said, "*To succeed, you must have tremendous perseverance, tremendous will. 'I will drink the ocean', says the persevering soul; 'at my will mountains will crumble up'. Have that sort of energy, that sort of will; work hard, and you will reach the goal.*" Unfortunately, we have limited ourselves without knowing our tremendous capabilities. We are stronger than we know. More beautiful than we think, worthier than we believe. So be strong, be confident and be you. If women are determined, there can be nothing impossible in the world!

Aurobindo Ghosh perceived that Vivekananda's influence is still working gigantically, we know not well how, we know not well where, in something that is not yet formed, something leonine, grand, intuitive, upheaving that has entered the soul of India and we say, "Behold, Vivekananda still lives in the soul of his Mother and in the souls of her children". The rise of outstanding women administrators, statesmen, scientists, writers and spiritual teachers, is gradually proving the truth of these prophetic words. Today Swami Vivekananda's words are proving true with the footsteps of Sarada Devi and Sister Nivedita. Women must come forward with a combination of the 'mother's heart and the hero's will,' a combination of the purity of Holy Mother and the dynamism of Rani of Jhansi or Joan of Arc.

Conclusion

"Swami Vivekananda was the epitome of all that was great and good in the India of the past. With Shankara's intellect, he combined Buddha's heart, Christ's renunciation, and the Prophet of Arabia's spirit of equality, and the result of this holy confluence will in time flood the whole world" -Swami Madhavmanda.

In order to Rejuvenate, Revitalize and Recharge the women of present era, Swami's inspiring words act as nectar to inculcate the spirit of freedom into the veins of the dynamic and active women of Mother India. Mindset is what needs to be changed and for this government, modes of entertainment and media and all the women have to play a major role. A girl can change a scenario. She is a mother hence, what she needs can be propagated in her child. Today's women have covered the distance from mother to manager: this is all what has empowered her. Swamiji always believed that everything that is happening around us, be it small, big, positive or negative, gives us the opportunity to manifest the potential within. He taught that we ought to live in this world like a lotus leaf, which grows in water but is never moistened by water; so a woman ought to live in the world—her heart to God and her hands to work.

WORK CITED

1. Kumari, Abhilasha & Sabina Kidwai. Crossing the Sacred Line: Women's Search for Political Power, Hyderabad: Orient Longman, 1998.

2. Letters of Swami Vivekananda. Calcutta: Advaita Ashrama, 1986.

3. Maithilyananda, Swami "The Ideal of Indian Womanhood", Vedanta Kesari, 1959.

4. Nair, Sukumaran. Swami Vivekananda: The Educator, New Delhi: Sterling Publishers, 1987.

5. Nivedita, Sister. The Master As I saw Him, Calcutta: Udbodhan Office, 1977.

6. Ranade, Eknath. Swami Vivekananda's Rousing Call to Hindu Nation, Calcutta: Century Publications, 1963.

7. Sharma, Radha Krishna. Nationalism, Social Reform and Indian Women, Patna: Janaki Prakasan, 1981.

8. The Complete Works of Swami Vivekananda. V, 2. Calcutta: Advaita Ashram, 1959.

9. V, 6. Cacutta: Advaita Ashrama, 1956.

10. V, 4. Calcutta: Advaita Ashrama, 1958.

11. V, 7. Calcutta: Advaita Ashrama, 1958.

12. V, 3. Calcutta: Advaita Ashrama, 1990.

13. V, 8. Calcutta: Advaita ashrama, 1990.

14. V, 5. Calcutta: Advaita Ashrama, 1997.

15. http://samyukta.info/site/user/login?destination=comment/reply/320% 2523comment-form

16. http://www.freeindia.org/biographies/vivekanand/page1.htm

17. http://kaustubh88.tripod.com/vivekananda/id33.html-quoat

❧ Chapter 16 ❧

Reforms of Swami Vivekananda on the Path of Tamil Siddhas

R. Ezhilraman

Ph.D. Research Scholar
Dept. of History
Pondicherry University

Introduction

Tamil siddhas are generally considered as an outcaste by the orthodox and elite groups of the Hindu society. However, in real these siddhas are the great reformers who brought too many progressive changes in the dog-tailed society. They also vehemently condemned the evil practices irrationally followed by the people in the name of their religion. Against these evils, the Tamil siddhas had sung hundreds of songs that created more revolution and reform in the society. We may proudly say that these Tamil siddhas are the pioneers of the social and religious reforms in India. In fact, every reformers and reforms in the modern India have at least the basic ideals and influence of these siddhas.

Similarly, like the Tamil siddhas, Swami Vivekananda (1863-1902) also too worked for the cause of social and religious reforms in the country. He directly or indirectly followed the ideals of the Tamil siddhas, against those social evils like caste, most particularly the bramanical influences in the society. He was too sharply critical of excesses perpetrated by the Brahmins in the name of rites, rituals, customs and religion as often cried by the siddhas. He himself accepted that the Tamil siddhas are great reformers and thus he started following their ideals to some extent. This chapter makes an attempt to correlate the social and religious reforms of Swami Vivekananda and how far he followed the path of the Tamil siddhas as they advocated in their songs.

Swami Vivekananda

As a well known fact, Swami Vivekananda was one among the greatest disciples of Sri Ramakrishna Paramahamsa. Vivekananda's real name was Narendranath Datta. He was born on 12th January 1863 in a middle class Kayastha family in Kolkata. He took the B.A. Degree of Calcutta University and became a keen student of both Eastern and Western Philosophy. Often he raises the question to any religious teacher whom he met that "Have You Seen God?" But none of them gave him a proper answer. One day he happened to meet Ramakrishna. Ramakrishna embraced him and told him, "I have been waiting for you for weeks and months and you have at last come"[1]. As usual Datta put forth the same question to Ramakrishna, "Have you seen God". Immediately Ramakrishna replied that "I have seen Him more clearly than I am seeing you now", "And if you so wish I can show him to you also"[2]. This too inspired Datta, who then after became a strong follower and disciple of Ramakrishna. Thus Datta considered Ramakrishna as his spiritual teacher and learnt his religious philosophy as well as various types of yogic practices associated with it[3].

His Interests in Vedanta and Philosophies

The great Tamil siddhas like Tirumular and Kaduvelicittar say that people should follow the Vedas[4]. Similarly, Narendranath Datta, who became a Sanyasin with Vivekananda as his pseudo name, got too interested in reading the *Vedas*, *Vedantas* and other philosophies. For some years he devoted himself to the study of *Vedanta* and other systems of philosophy along with his friends who also became *sanyasins*. It is said that, just before his death, Ramakrishna called Datta and told him that, "You are not an ordinary man. You are God Narayana Himself and it is now your duty to devote all your life to teach not only the people of India but also the people of the whole world the Supreme value of Vedanta". Datta promised to do so, and became a *sanyasin* along with many of his friends. Thus they founded the Ramakrishna Mutt to carry on the propaganda on the lines laid down by his master, Ramakrishna[5].

The Parliament of Religions, 1893

Vivekananda heard of a meeting of the Parliament of Religions in 1893 at Chicago in USA and participated in it. Unlike other delegates who spoke in praise of their own religions, he spoke of the Vedanta which stood for equality of all religions. This impressed the large audience and many American papers wrote editorials in his praise. Thus he became a celebrity in USA. He spent four years in that country, visiting all the cities and also established many Vedanta centres in those cities. From America he went to England and to several European countries carrying the message of the Vedanta and revised their views on the nature of Indian civilisation and culture. In 1897, he returned to India. Then after, he spent most of his time for the development of the downtrodden and called on his countrymen to remove poverty and untouchability[6].

Siddhas: the Unselfish Social Reformers

A siddha is one who has attained perfection or *siddhi* by means of yogic practice[7]. They are the authors of a distinct and well organised type of religious, philosophic and mystic poetry in Tamil[8]. Popularly there are eighteen siddhas[9] in Tamil tradition known as '*Pathinēn Siddhars*'. They were the founders (and authors) of a popular literature that is best characterized in negative terms: anti-establishment, anti-ritual, anti-caste, anti-Brahmin, non-devotional, relativistic and pessimistic[10]. They were wandering tantric adepts who sang in rough popular idiom about the abuses of society, the glory of God, and the need to seek freedom and immortality by means of yogic practices[11]. Apart from these, they are good guides and real gurus in the sense that a good teacher will emphasize practice and personal experience, who worked for the cause of the society and silently made several reforms in the society.

Vivekananda's idea on Social Reform

No reformer in this country and to some extent in this world, would directly or indirectly not followed the ideals of the Tamil siddhas in their reforms that they thought to bring in the society and religion. Similarly Swami Vivekananda was also influenced and inspired by the ideals of the siddhas and other Tamil saints who worked for the cause of the society without any political or economical benefits. In one of his lectures Vivekananda himself says that, 'The modern types of reform, which are really not worth the name, as they are indulged in by some educated people and some plutocrats merely to hoodwink the innocent common man. They are not calculated to improve his lot⊡ the principal reason for this state of affairs is that the people who are really responsible for the degradation of the masses have come out as reformers for purely political reasons. But the reformers I have in mind are the great siddhas, Buddha, Thiruvalluvar, Ramanuja, and the like who were reputed to have attempted social reform but yet failed miserably'[12]. Further he also points out to the other reformers that, 'To the reformers I will point out that I am a greater reformer than any one of them. They want to reform only little bits. I want root and branch reform. Thiers is the method of destruction, mine is that of construction. Most of the reforms that have been agitated for during the past century have been ornamental. Every one of these reforms only touches the first two castes and no other'[13]. True to this fact, the Tamil siddhas also mostly touched Brahmin groups and their practices as the main social evils.

Vivekananda against Caste, Religion and Scriptures

The most important item of social reform in our country refers to the inequality based on birth... It is impossible to say that any reform was done by our reformers genuinely for the benefit of the masses. The obstruction posed by belief in God, religion, Vedas, Shastras is the main reason for the lack of any initiative of effort on the part of our reformers. However, the divisions in Indian society have benefited and still benefit certain castes who have all along turned a deaf ear to all talk of reform...[14]

In order to jolt people out of their intellectual rut and their conventional thinking, the Tamil siddhas have vehemently criticised the *puranas*, the *Vedas* and the *Sastras*. Swami Vivekananda used to compare the readers of many *sastras* but who do not understand the real meaning of them as assess carrying a library of books. As Sivavakkiyar says, they are like the spoons that are used for different cooking operations, but yet remain without a single taste of the food they prepare. The Tamil siddhas do not recognise distinction among various religions, and also they do not accept the various caste distinctions in society. Bhadragiriyar dreams of a future age when there would be no caste. On behalf of all the Tamil siddhas, Kakapusundar says that they will not have or entertain any caste distinction whatsoever. Pampatticittar is so angry with caste hierarchy that he wants to burn it down. Sivavakkiyar scoffs at the upholders of caste system and violently opposes the practice of untouchability by raising a pertinent question whether the bones, flesh and skin of an upper-caste woman and those of a lower-caste woman with reference to the above are distinguishable on the basis of caste? By rising a question of what caste is, Sivavakkiyar denies the objective reality of it. He takes the Brahmin as a symbol of the upholders of caste system and criticises Brahmanism vehemently through his songs[15].

In the same way, unselfishness and the social responsibilities of religion are ideas that are strongly underlined in the life and activities of Swami Vivekananda. On the other hand, the Swami also reinforced the thesis that religion could not be judged by the purely rational or utilitarian needs of society. Vivekananda saw society and social developments to be by their very nature unstable and transitory[16]. Above all, the real aim of the siddha criticism of higher caste is to show that the doors of yoga have always been open to all castes and classes, to all men and women irrespective of their birth, upbringing, tradition, culture or education. At the hands of the siddhas, *yoga* has become India's primary tool for self-reconciliation in the face of society's contrary pulls[17]. Therefore, Swami Vivekananda was also too interested in practicing as well as in propagating *yoga*.

Importance of Yoga

Yoga Sadhana is one of the basic practice in tantric cult. Through the *yoga sadhana* the human body is to be made strong and thus the mental plane is also strengthened. This will ultimately give the *Sadhaka* the needed physical and mental pre-requisite for the attaiment of *Kaya Siddhi*. It is a *sadhana*, a method, a technique or a path. One may have faith in any religion. One can practice or do *sadhana* as it does not touch one's religion or faith. It is a regulated path to bring God, the deities and others under one's control through worship and prayer. It contains various methods of *sadhana* and use of materials in specified forms, under set rules and directions[18].

To the genuine siddha, the extremely arduous discipline of *yoga* leading to the awakening of the *kundalini sakti* is the only source of the real accomplishment of *siddhis*[19]. Probably the Tamil siddhas are called 'eighteen siddhas' and are also known as *Maha Siddhas* because they have in their *kundalini yoga*, crossed these eighteen *mahavidyas*[20]. In this connection, on one occasion, it would be of interest to note that in comparing Swami Vivekananda with other spiritual luminaries of his time, Sri Ramakrishna said of him: "If Keshub Chandra Sen had one power which made him famous, Vivekananda had eighteen such powers in the fullest measure..."[21] As Swami Vivekananda has said *siddhis* are milestones on the way to spiritual progress. Further, *siddhis* are not contrary to nature. They appear to be supernatural since the normal man does not care to cultivate them. According to *karma-yoga* of the Bhagavad Gita, *naiskarmyam* and siddha connote the same—that is, the state of perfection[22].

His Raja-yoga and Karma-yoga

A revival of Patanjali's yoga began at the end of the nineteenth century, when the Yoga Sutra was translated and commented on by Swami Vivekananda. He called his book *Raja-Yoga*, one of many names by which the yoga of Patanjali is known. His reading of the text was strongly influenced by the Vedanta philosophy, of which he was a great modern proponent[23].

In genuine siddha mysticism of Tamil Nadu, humanity and not God, is the point of reference. The *karma-yoga* is also based on the principle of serving the people. Very often, St. Ramalinga, a 19th century Tamil siddha advocates to serve for the cause of the needy, by which one can see the God in the smile of the poor. In fact, after realisation, the siddha does not withdraw himself from society, but works for the welfare of the people out of deep compassion. At this level, ethical precepts flow out of the realised being and they serve as guide-posts for others for better living[24].

Similarly Ramakrishna also advocated that, 'not mercy, but service, service for man, must be regarded as God'. Vivekananda institutionalised Ramakrishna's ideals of social service. And as stated above, he surprised America by his eloquent and lucid presentation of Vedanta and Hinduism at the Parliament of Religions at Chicago in 1893 and on other platforms. He had more to do with South India than his *guru* and spent some time in the city of Madras (present Chennai) on different occasions. He organised the Ramakrishna Mission, for the regeneration of Hinduism and for social work both in India and abroad. The Mission runs a mutt, a student's home, a college and several high schools in Chennai. Vivekananda laid stress on the broad basis of Hinduism, its tolerance and catholicity[25].

Conclusion

Like above reforms, there exist many to say about Swami Vivekananda in comparison with the socio-religious reforms of Tamil siddhas. In many ways, he followed the path of Tamil siddhas. To some extent, it is said that he also indulged in practicing the *kunda-*

lini yoga like a siddha. Though he was considered as a great *sanyasin*, most of his spiritual practices are similar to the siddha tradition. As a well known fact, most of the tantric practitioners and siddhas are the worshippers of *Shakti*, the feminine power. Similarly, followed by Ramakrishna, Vivekananda was also a follower of Kali. Kali is the most popular deity in Bengal. 'Ramakrishna Paramahamsa is said to have visualised the goddess, and made his disciple, Vivekananda, see Her'[26]. Besides, like a realised siddha, Swami Vivekananda frequently refers to 'the joy that never spoke'. Since it is a state of completeness or wholeness, there is no scope for any action. As Tirumular says, the moment he has attained this state of *jnana*, he becomes actionless. He calls such people 'men without action' or in Tamil *Sombar*. It is not a state of idleness or laziness, or inactivity, but a state of Siddhahood, which is the 'occupation of all occupations'[27].

Thus, in many aspects, the ideas and ideals of Swami Vivekananda is similar to the ideals of Tamil siddhas. In short span of life, he tirelessly worked for the development of the society, religion, particularly Hinduism, and for the poor people. But, this nonstop and untiring work led to a breakdown of his health and he passed away prematurely at the young age of thirty nine in 1902. However he is still living among us for his work as a social and religious reformer. Thus he has obtained a place of permanence in the country. Many of the educational and philanthropic institutions are running in his name. One can witness his statues in every state of the country, particularly, his statues at the tip of the Indian Ocean at Kanyakumari and in the India Gate at Mumbai deserves the attention of many people who gather there.

NOTES AND REFERENCES

1. Alladi Vaidehi Krishnamurthy, *Freedom Movement in India: 1857 and After*, Neelkamal Publications Pvt. Ltd., New Delhi, 2010, p. 43 (Henceforth A. Vaidehi)

2   Swami Lokeswarananda, *Ramakrishna Paramahamsa*, Sahitya Academy, New Delhi, 1997, p. 38

3   A. Vaidehi, *op.cit*, p. 43

4.   *Tirumandiram,* Verse 51 and *Kaduveli Siddhar Songs,* Verse 8

5.   A. Vaidehi, *op.cit,* p. 43

6.   *Ibid,* pp. 43-45

7.   Peter Heehs, (Ed.), *Indian Religion: The Spiritual Traditions of South India,* Permanent Black, New Delhi, (2006), 2002, p. 282.

8.   R. Champakalakshmi, 'From Devotion and Dissent to Dominance: The Bhakti of the Tamil Alvars and Nayanars', in David N. Lorenzen (Ed.), *Religious Movements in South Asia 600-1300 A.D.,* OUP, New Delhi, 2005, p. 60

9.   Regarding their total number, there prevail a tradition of the 'Eighteen Siddhas', which credited with wisdom, supernatural powers and knowledge of medicine, alchemy, mantras etc. But in real, there exist a number of lists of these eighteen Siddhas, but none resembles other.

10. The best known of these Siddhas are Sivavakkiyar, Pattinattar, and Pāmpāṭṭic-Cittar.

11. Peter Heehs, (Ed.), *op.cit.* p. 283

12. Excerpted from Swami Vivekananda, 'The Mission of the Vedanta' and 'My Plan of Campaign', quoted in Amiya P. Sen (ed.,), *Social and Religious Reform: The Hindus of British India,* OUP, New Delhi, 2005, p. 68 (Henceforth Sen)

13. Sen, *op.cit,* p. 69

14. *Ibid,* p. 69

15. T.N. Ganapathy, *The Philosophy of the Tamil Siddhas,* Indian Council for Philosophical Research, New Delhi, 2nd Edn., 2004, pp. 192-194

16. Swami Vivekananda, 'Notes of Class Talks and Lectures: The Complete Works of Swami Vivekananda' quoted in Sen, *op.cit,* p. 15

17. T.N. Ganapathy, *op.cit,* p. 197

18. L. R. Chawdhri, *Secrets of Yantra, Mantra and Tantra,* New Dawn Press, INC., New Delhi, 1992, P. 121

19. T.N. Ganapathy, *op.cit,* p. 52

20. *Ibid,* p. 26

21. E.R. Marozzi, "The Making of Swami Vivekananda", in *Swami Vivekananda in East and West,* The Ramakrishna Centre, London, 1968, p. 11

22. T.N. Ganapathy, *op.cit,* p. 53

23. Peter Heehs, (Ed.), *op.cit*, p. 137

24. T.N. Ganapathy, *op.cit*, pp. 197-198

25. K.A. Nilakanta Sastri, *Development of Religion in South India*, Munshiram Manoharlal Publishers Pvt. Ltd., New Delhi, 1992, p. 137

26. S.C. Banerji, *A Brief History of Tantra Literature*, Naya Prokash, Calcutta, 1988, p. 472

27. T.N. Ganapathy, *op.cit*, pp. 154-155

Chapter 17

Women Education and Social Changes in the 19th Century Bengal

R. Lakshmi,

M. Phil Scholar
Department of History K.M.C.P.G.S,
Puducherry.

Introduction

"Educate your women first and leave them to themselves;

Then they will tell you what reforms are necessary for them".

Swami Vivekananda

During the 19th century, Bengal had witnessed a spurt of reforms centering round the status of women, who were so long neglected by the society and kept in seclusion. Women were bounded by social constraints like, sati, female infanticide, child marriage, slavery, purdah system, dowry system, etc. Women were assigned a secondary status, considered a weaker sex and relegated to the position of a helpless section of the society. Their whole life was confined to the four walls of the Hindu tradition, which was dogmatic in fashion with strict implications designed in the religions. Social and religious practices were regressive of women's emancipation. It was really tragic that women of our country seldom realize their own significance as builders of the nation due to the lack of education. To offer a way out of this ignorant position 'a clarion call for women' was given by Swami Vivekananda. He emphasized education as a precondition for the cause of women's emancipation and it would bring an all-round development in the society. The most visible contribution of Vivekananda is the establishment of the Ramakrishna Mission and altogether he gave a new direction to the role of sanyasins for imparting secular education to all women through his spiritual knowledge of Vedantic Socialism. The main purpose of this chapter is to expound the contributions of Swami Vivekananda and his chosen disciple Sister Nivedita to the women's education, particularly in the 19th and 20th century India, as a basic parameter for the social changes and development in India. This work is based on the secondary sources collected from the government libraries.

Historical Retrospect of Women Education

It is accepted, generally, that the best way to judge the pattern and direction of social change in a country is to find out the condition of its women. Rig Vedic women enjoyed complete equality on par with men. They had considerable freedom of right to education. In the later Vedic period, women were gradually deprived of their status that they had enjoyed in the Rig Vedic Age. They were withheld from studying Vedas and also restricted to attend Vedic Assemblies. Medieval Age in Indian History was a period of Muslim invasions, continuously upsetting the traditional social institutions, with vast migration of people, and prolonged unsettlement. All these resulted in a sense of insecurity for the people and it became a need of the hour to keep women protected from invading strangers. This gradually settled down as a custom and the position of women in India deteriorated. Consequently, the increasing number of child marriages took place. Practices like sati... left no room for women to think in terms of her individual status. Her status both in life and death was tagged to her husband, to her son and her father. Added to these, women were not allowed to get education.[1] The advent of British marked a new phase in the women education in India. The various socio-religious reform movement tried to awaken the conscience of people against certain obnoxious social practices.[2]

Impression of Vivekananda

Swami Vivekananda was a great intellectual, vedantic, philosopher, patriot-monk, and above all he was a philanthropist. As a philanthropist, he extended his attention and admiration towards Indian women. He wanted to enlighten them through education. He openly advocated women education and he himself produced scholarly women through his teachings, one of them was Sister Nivedita. He was an active social reformer and an impassioned contributor to the Renaissance of the 19th century Bengal. An important problem of the time of Vivekananda was the low social status of Indian women. He exclaimed, "It is very difficult to understand why in this country so much difference is made between men and women, whereas the Vedanta declares that one and the same conscious self is present in all beings." He always maintained that women education was completely essential not only for emancipation of women, but also for the upliftment of society as a whole.[3]

There were three distinct strands that can be discerned in the pattern of reaction of the *bhadralok* intelligentsia to the western impact. They were conservatives, reformists and radicals. In this category, Vivekananda belongs to the second one. His ideal of reform was based on improving the condition of women, and introduction of women education. 'A country could not progress by neglecting its womenfolk, just as a bird could not fly without one of its wings', said Swami Vivekananda. In India, illiterate women, the sure 'victims of ennui', they now became 'passive objects of reform'. Realizing the limitations of such man-sponsored reforms, Vivekananda observed, "Women will work out their own destinies much better too, than men can ever do for them. All the mischief to women has come because men undertook to shape the destiny of women."[4] In a letter to his brother disciple Swami Ramakrishnananda, Vivekananda wrote that, "There is no chance for the welfare of the world unless the condition of women is improved... In India there are two great evils, trampling the women, and grinding the poor through caste restrictions."[5] Society permitted man to have rights and freedom from which women were excluded and different standards were adopted to judge the individual and conduct of man and woman. To Vivekananda it seemed absurd to complain that knowledge was not given to women. Vivekananda was evidently not a blind patriot nor was he an upholder of the status-quo in social relations or social institutions. He wanted fresh air to blow in and he wanted the individual to awake and assert himself. He knew that social change could not come about without the stimulus of individual thought; and that was why he advocated an educational system that would develop the thinking power rather than an accumulation of knowledge and would promote manliness and freedom from fear rather than conformity and superstition-induced behaviour. Vivekananda was also aware that while intellectual development may stimulate change, change would not get implemented without mass education. It was his love for the country and the desire to see it change in the right direction that led him to undertake a fearless analysis of its national weaknesses of character and organization.[6]

According to Vivekananda, Education is for the benefit of all people without any discrimination, which makes a person to understand his society and people. We want a man-making education, which should be utilized in the service of poor and suffering humanity. Work for them and that will be the real service to God.[7] There were two incidents to prove his sympathetic ideal of education, one is Swami Vivekananda himself undertook tour of the country passing through various vicissitudes of poverty, starvation and other forms of privation. He was greatly pained by the plight of the poor in India. Another is when he went to the Parliament of Religions at Chicago his address beginning with "Brothers and Sisters of America" created a tremendous impression on the audience and every time he began to speak he was listened to with rapt attention and greeted with thundering applause. But when he returned to his place of stay after the first day's session the dominant emotion in his mind was not one of exultation. He could not sleep during the night conscious of the wide contrast between the prosperity of the American people and the poverty and starvation of the common man in India. He wept over the misery of the poor in India and prayed to the Mother Goddess, "O Mother! What do I care for name and fame, when my mother-land remains sunk in utmost poverty...? Who will raise the masses of India? Who will give them bread? O, Mother! Show me the way to help them!" This thereafter became the core of his educational philosophy and reason for the development of the heart-deep sympathy, which will feel for the people, the poor, the sick and the downtrodden. So, that the educated will devote all their strength and might in their service. To achieve this daunting task he advocated life-building and man-making education which will assimilate ideas to build character.[8]

Vivekananda also emphasized the importance of the teacher winning his pupil through personal interest and affection and building up his self-confidence. He felt himself able to do great things because of the confidence that his Master showed in his ability and integrity and the love that he showered upon him. His own life was a wonderful example of what an ideal teacher can do to a difficult disciple. He knew that self-confidence was more than half the secret of success in life and it required careful and sympathetic nurturing at an early age.[9] The great emphasis that he laid in his teachings on education was the prime importance of taking it to the masses particularly to the rural masses. He asserted that "the chief cause of India's ruin has been the monopolizing of the whole education and intelligence of the land, by dint of pride and royal authority among a handful of men."[10]

Vivekananda undoubtedly stimulated women education especially in India and became a symbol of national pride as the one who had successfully stood up to the West and made it acknowledge him as Master. He took pride in the country's inheritance from the past: at the same time, he was not an obscurantist revivalist with undiscriminating admiration for all that had come down from the past. He held the view that customs and life styles had a very definite link with the times and circumstances under which they came into existence and had to be changed with the passing of time and the changing of circumstances. Thus, the system of education had to be changed to bring it in line with the original values of the *Vedanta*. His other sphere of influence on modern India should have been his ideas on education. He recognized the difficulty of poor women in rural areas in attending school education. In fact, the idea he conceived of itinerant teachers of secular knowledge, he of course devised it principally for the *sanyasins* whom he wanted to take to the path of service which is a most practical way of both rousing interest in adult illiterates and giving rural adults some rudiments of modern knowledge, still remain to be taken up by Governments, let alone implemented on any significant scale. He can also be given credit for pioneering the idea of industrial training and technical education which have now become a part of the educational system of modern India. His particular stress on making educational facilities for women in villages is also worth remembering. He definitely rejected the concept of education as an information-oriented and memory-filling process. He believed that education should aim at developing the mind rather than stuff it with book knowledge. He wanted education of both men and women to include all aspects of life, not only the intellectual, but also the physical, cultural, social and spiritual and the adoption of a fearless and self-reliant attitude towards life. Vivekananda believed that "the best thermometer" to the progress of a nation is its treatment of its women and affirmed that the Hindu religion does not at all prevent women being educated and that the old books had shown that the universities were equally resorted to by both girls and boys and India had a unique record of women saints and expositors in its religious history. [11]

The first Bengali work on women education titled *Strisiksa Vidhayak*, authored by Pandit Gaurmohon Vidyalankar, was published in 1822. 'The *Strisiksa Vidhayak* stressed that women education did not mean greater freedom of behaviour, nor did it over-ride a woman's primary duty to her husband. It was assumed that women would only be interested in education to enhance their wife-mother role'. This conservatism gripped the psyche of the *bhadralok*, subject to pressure from two sides. This was severely opposed by Vivekananda. Because, the educated women of the nineteenth century Bengal themselves fashioned the traditional ideal of 'self-renunciation' of the 'incorruptibly good' wife or mother. As always these women too absorbed the ideal, compounded out of approved stereotypic qualities like loyalty to the husband, dedication, sacrifice and commitment in discharging duties, and the enormous responsibility of motherhood. They were socialised into accepting this ideal which defined their sanctioned role in society. To change this social deprivation of women, Vivekananda stressed the importance of women education to realize the cherished ideals of dedication and commitment in discharging duties in a better and more effective way. [12]In his words, "True Education is that by which character is formed, strength of mind is increased, intellect is expanded, by which on can stand on one's own feet".[13] He felt that there was an urgent need to assimilate the spirit of science, so that Indian education would become a blend of Vedanta and modern science. At Swami Vivekananda's behest the Ramakrishna Mission runs more than thirty five educational institutions in different parts of the country.

Education on secular line will lead a way to bring socialism, as it is an essential prerequisite for a social change. More importantly women education would make them aware of their present condition and also would give them an idea as to how to solve their problem both in home and in society. [14]Vivekananda regarded education as the panacea or a sure means, to bring about our national regeneration, through the upliftment of women. He believed education would bring about an all-round socio-economic, physical, moral and spiritual development of women and not merely help her adjust to her needs and habits. "If the condition of women is raised, the benefit will be surely seen in the well-being of their children to the lasting good of the whole Indian society."[15] His concept of an 'ideal' or elevated woman, with the fullest development of her inherent qualities called for a synthesis of the eternal spiritual values of India with the modern values of life. A woman's *math* was established for the dissemination of this balanced education. Such a *math* would be a residential institution with provision for admitting day scholars. The *brahmacharinis* will open centers of education in villages and towns and strive for the spread of women education. [16]

With regard to the curriculum to be followed, he prescribed the study of religion, Sanskrit, English and other languages, literature (excluding novels and fictions), history, Puranas, science, acquiring a range of domestic skills (housekeeping, sewing, culinary art, hygiene and the up-bringing of children), physical training (particularly training in self-defence), painting, photography, origami, service to humanity and all living creatures and vocational training. Swami Vivekananda believed that "Each individual is the external expression of an ideal society of a nation"[17], this individualism developed only through education. The great question of the day was that of education and it was to be the turning point in the woman education.

To sum up Vivekananda's ideas on education, its main base was his faith in the youth of the country for national regeneration. Hence his anxiety that they should get the right type of education and also goes about the right way for getting the best out of education. Asked to define his idea of right education, he answered: "I never define anything. Still it may be described as a development of faculty, not an accumulation of words, but a training of individuals to will rightly and efficiently." He wanted man-making education for the young and he wanted such educated young man to use their education to make men out of others. And when he talked of men, he included women also. Use of the intellect rather than accumulation of information, concentration rather than memorizing, integrated development of the human personality in the ascending scale of body, mind and heart, cultivation of fearlessness in pursuit of truth and compassion and fraternity in dealing with fellow-men, science instead of superstition, rationality in place of obscurantism, and absorption of the spirited message of the Vedanta that all men are divine and it only needs will, strength and effort to realize their divinity, and in the process recognize the common bond that makes all humanity kin—this is the message that Vivekananda gives to those who give or seek education. Vivekananda said that women who were the victims of oppression were like vixen. Only with educational opportunity could they become 'lionesses'. Revealing the true nature of their strength, he sought to channelize the benefits of education to all the members of society and to develop their lost individuality. "Only let Women and the People achieve education!" was his earnest plea.[18]

Impression of Nivedita

An Anglo-Irish disciple of Vivekananda was Margaret Elizabeth Noble or Sister Nivedita as she came to be known later. She met Vivekananda in 1895 and was inspired to settle in Kolkata and worked for the women's emancipation. After her arrival in Kolkata on 28 January 1898, Nivedita pursued initiation into the neo-traditional, Hindu monastic community founded by Ramakrishna and then led by Vivekananda. Her motto of education is "Mutual Aid, Self-reliance, and Co-operation". In the words of Sister Nivedita, "There is nothing which is more necessary socially than education". According to Nivedita, as women are the strength of the family and central to its life, status of women must begin with the study of the social framework. Social structures, cultural norms and value systems determines to a great extent, a woman's roles and her position in society. In determining their status, Nivedita has dealt with their education. Ancient women used to get education worth the name and fame while the medieval conception had assigned women to domestic duties. She said that a new type of education and new ideals were necessary for women. But the new ideals had to be approached through the old, and the unfamiliar had to be approached through the familiar. "Discussing how this could be achieved, she said, when the women see themselves in their true place, as related to the soil on which they live; when they become aware of the needs of their own people...." A sound education of Indian women must begin and end into exaltation of the national ideals of womanhood. It was by learning of one's own past that the future could be realized. But, how was this to be achieved in the field of woman's education?[19]

Nivedita was convinced that the Indian woman would herself educate other Indian women and their education must be modernized to have a wider outlook than before. According to her, home was to be the window through which the world was to be seen. The school and the home, according to her, were equally necessary. In an ideal education they act and react upon one another. Nivedita considered education of the Indian women to be largely a discipline rather than a development. The second great educational factor in a woman's life was embedded in the mythological social culture of the past.

The future of Indian woman depended on the type of education she received. Woman had to learn to be human and the barriers to her development had to be removed. The value of education, according to Nivedita, was not individual but social and communal. And education was partly a question of social adjustment. Education should render the individual fit for her society. According to her, the moral ideal of India had taken new dimensions—the national and the civic. Women should be educated in the form best suited to needs of the country. In fact, women in villages were not accustomed to think of much larger areas than the village. However they were not without their own civic centers and gathering places. They, therefore, must be trained to play her part.[20]Her efforts not only culminated in the present well-known Nivedita Girls' school at Kolkata but also paved the way for the foundation of a number of other educational institutions, including a first-grade college run by the Ramakrishna Sarada Mission, Dakshineswar. Nivedita's school was established in Nov 1898 with the encouragement of Swami Vivekananda and aimed to provide instruction in English and in the vernacular language of Bengal. Subjects included elementary science, literature, mathematics and handicrafts with a special bearing on the revival of the traditional Indian industries. The object of including handicrafts was to enable 'every pupil to earn her own living and to create self-employment. Though she was interested in the comparative methods of the Swiss educational reformer Johann Heinrich Pestalozzi and German educationist Friedrich Froebel, she adopted and applied her Master's idea on education in her school.[21]

In the Colonial India, literacy was generally more pronounced among the higher income group than among middle class and lower middle class families, the latter groups being the most conservative sections in society. The task before Nivedita who targeted the latter group was indeed very challenging, she had to not only bring the *pardanashins* (women in seclusion) from their close seclusion to the liberated environment of a school, but being a foreigner had also to imbibe the ethos of this class. Her sincerity of purpose, simple and austere way of living and line of 'least resistance' to the existing institutions gradually broke down the barriers of social orthodoxy and racial antipathy.[22]

Regarding the formative phase of the evolution of her school, she made the following observation—"To myself it was clear that the school, when opened, must at first be only tentative and experimental. I had to learn what was wanted, to determine where I myself stood, to explore the very world of which my efforts were to become a part. The one thing that I knew was that an educational effort must begin at the stand point of the learner, and help to develop in own way. But I had no definite plans of which would be qualitatively true and universally applicable to the work of modern education of Indian women." Nivedita started her school in 1898 in a dingy alley of Bag Bazaar. But without a proper classroom, equipment or strong financial backing her task became increasingly difficult. So within seven months she had to wind up her school and go abroad to collect funds for her venture. The school was restarted in 1902 with professional support of Sister Christine, another disciple of Vivekananda. The curriculum included reading, writing, sewing and interpreting the lives of great religious leaders. As the number of children dwindled with the passage of time, they thought it prudent to start a women's section along with it, from 12 to 14 in the afternoon. This section immediately caught the fancy of the women in seclusion and the response was so overwhelming. That on the opening day itself some 60 ladies attended the school and the carriage could not be sent to fetch girls from more families for want of accommodation. Strict purdah was maintained within the school. As the number of women students increased, a separate section called the *Pura-stri Vibhaga* was started in 1904.[23]

Unlike any other girls schools of this time which stressed upon 'domestic education for girls' in contrast to 'academic education for boys', the Nivedita School, from the very beginning stressed upon the necessity to teach at least one 'craft'-based subject. This was done to enable every pupil to earn her own living, if necessary, without leaving her home, by a pursuit which was to be wholly ennobling. So, along with tailoring and sewing, knitting, spinning and weaving were introduced as the last items for a brief period. Moreover, teaching as a career, encouraged opening of new avenues for young widows. For these would-be teachers, the syllabus included Bengali, History Arithmetic, English, Geography, Sanskrit, Geometry, brush work, needle work and kindergarten methods. Thus students of this school were able to earn by knitting, sewing and teaching. A few of them even became school mistresses of exceptional ability, earning Rs.40 to Rs.50 per month even in those days.[24]

In accordance with the decision of Sister Nivedita to refrain from taking any help from the alien government, the school functioned without any government financial aid. This policy was judiciously followed till India attained independence in 1947. Consequently, the school had to depend mainly on donations from the public, as well as the money obtained by Sister Nivedita through her writings and lectures, and by Sister Christine through teaching outside. But this amount was never very substantial. As such, the school functioned through financial strains. Teachers were mainly honorary and past pupils of the school often taught with a nominal monthly allowance. Nivedita decided to further the cause of women's upliftment. After her demise in 1911 the school was for a short time run by Sister Christine. With the establishment of the Home, the seed of Vivekananda nunnery was sown and Nivedita's dream of training educational missionaries was realized. In 1918, the school was affiliated to the Ramakrishna Mission and came to be known as the Ramakrishna Mission Sister Nivedita Girls School. The high ideal of service, both of the school and of the students' home, made it a unique and highly respected institution. An officer of the Calcutta Police Special Branch in his Report, (dated 13th February, 1923) on the school, observed, 'It is the best institution for real *Pardanashin* girls, women and widows of Hindu families. It is a free institution under the management of the Ramakrishna Mission. It teaches the students Bengali, History, Geography, Mathematics, English, Sanskrit, needle work, tailoring, knitting, spinning, etc. It lays a great stress on moral training from the Ramayan, the Mahabharata, the Vedanta doctrines and the lives of great religious leaders.[25]

The present teachers had got their training in this school and followed the noble example of the Sister Nivedita in devoting their lives to the cause of the school without taking any remuneration. Its expenses are met from funds available from the friends and patrons of the Mission both in India and in America. It has no connection with any political party. Its education and training produce qualified female characters who not only become fit to maintain themselves in case of emergency but become all the more amiable in their behaviour in family and society, which is the true object of this institute.'

We may say that motherhood, wifehood and widowhood were viewed by Nivedita in their ideal forms, pertaining to which the individual played her role in society. Often, the different roles were played by the same woman at different times. Education for women was emphasized so that they may become aware of their position and participate in the development of the nation. Thus, though the age-old traditions, attitudes and practices take long to die, there is perceptible change in the role and status of Indian women. The status of women can be realized only through education particularly in rural areas. The civic evolution of woman as a process, to Nivedita's thinking, takes place most rapidly in those communities and in those epochs when political or industrial transformation, or both are at their heights. The marked tendency of modern nations towards the economic independence of woman had hastened the process.[26] Nivedita holds out the Messianic hope to all men in stating that "the education of all, the people as well as the classes, woman as well as man, is not to be a desire with us, but lies upon us as a command". With these words Nivedita holds wide open the gate for the education of women to produce a greater society.[27] India is a heaven with all fortunes, if all Indians have access to vedantic or universal or secular education. There is no disparity among human to human.

Concluding Remarks

Why women education is important for social changes and national development? Answer for all these questions is the same which is according to our Indian tradition—women is the sole responsible for bringing up a child as a good human for future world. However, the position of Indian women and their status was lower when compared to the women in the western world. The institution of marriage, relating to the system of child marriage, polygamy and the *Kulin* Brahman marriage, and parents when unable to marry off their daughters, as a result marrying them to Gods (making them prostitutes), had all been targets of attack of Vivekananda. So he called Nivedita who in turn deals with them each in turn. It is a social progress of human life in which education exerts its influence on society and society on education. Education has opened up an arena in which women can compete freely with men and prove themselves. It has brought women out of the confines of the home and put them into contact with the philosophy of liberation and the democratic traditions of the West. It has expanded the role of women in Indian society beyond their traditional roles. This is particularly true for the middle strata of the society in which education has been taken up as a mark of social respectability and also as an instrument of economic gain.

According to the changing perspectives of women education in India, today every home is buffeted by winds of change from all directions. Women are becoming aware of their rights and they will have to assert themselves to change their position in society and to enjoy the rights, given to them by the constitution. This will greatly depend on "whether the Indian women has the wisdom and discrimination to distinguish between what to respect and what to reject; whether she is able to achieve a harmonious synthesis between the best of our traditions and the most desirable of the modern."[28] Women education in rural India is still at a low level while as regards the inclusion of spirituality in their education, it is still to be accomplished. The great deal of our nationalizing women's education during the coming years leads to making the women of our families more devoted to the development of the country. Women must acquire an enlarged idea of public life and be aware of the needs of their own people. This is what Swami Vivekananda wished, even though he died, but his soul remains within every human beings.

Today of course, women education has given them their rightful place; but in actual fact, women's education in rural India is still at a low level, while as regards the inclusion of spirituality in their education, it is still to be accomplished. So here again, while Vivekananda has influenced the making of modern India, what has been achieved is still far below what he preached. Altogether he gave a new direction to the role of *brahmacharinis* like Sister Nivedita. For the first time in the Indian History, we have woman *sanyasins* who dedicated their whole lives to the women's emancipation and social development in India.

Political institution and its mechanism in our country are necessary in making women education more successful and in that matter the co-operation of every citizen is also equally important. It is possible only when equal opportunity to all will be provided on the scale of educational merit and economic backwardness. Particularly in the slum areas of India, people are suffering for their livelihood. Women are the victims of everyday harassment both physically and mentally in all walks of their life for one reason or the other which is unimaginable in the post-independent India. The best solution for all these problems is good education. The purpose and meaning of man-making education is fulfilled only by imparting moral and value education to both men and women. It ultimately leads to the nation-making education, which was the dream of Vivekananda, well accomplished by his disciple Sister Nivedita.

NOTES AND REFERENCES

1. Seth, Padma, 'The status of women and Their Legal Rights', in *The Journal of India Education*, Nov.1975, vol.I, No.4, NCERT, p.29.

2. Agarwal, Mamta, *op.cit.*, p.30.

3. Rao, V.K.R.V, *Swami Vivekananda*, New Delhi, 1979, p.231.

4. C.W., vol. VIII, p.91.

5   C.W., vol. VI, pp.328-335.

6   Bordia, K.L., *Perspectives in Indian Education*, New Delhi, 1992, pp45-46.

7   Rao, V.K.R.V, *Swami Vivekananda*, New Delhi, 1979, p.187.

8   Bordia, K.L., *Perspectives in Indian Education*, pp.43-44.

9   Rao, V.K.R.V, *Swami Vivekananda*, pp.182-183.

10 Report of the Committee on the Status of women in India, p.76.

11 Rao, V.K.R.V, *Swami Vivekananda*, p.245.

12 Sengupta, Kalyan, & Bandyopadhyay, Tirthanath, (ed.), *The 19th Century Thought in Bengal*, Calcutta, 1998, pp.188-193.

13 Bordia, K.L., *op.cit.*, p.44.

14 Nikhilananda, Swami, (ed.), *Swami Vivekananda on India and her Problems*, Calcutta, 1982, p.132.

15 *Ibid.*, p.76.

16 Rao, V.K.R.V, *Swami Vivekananda*, New Delhi, 1979, pp.244-245.

17 Mukherjee, Santana, *Sister Nivedita in Search of Humanity*, Calcutta, 1997, p.43.

18 *Ibid.*, p.178.

19 *Ibid.*, p.50.

20 Mukherjee, Santana, *Sister Nivedita in Search of Humanity*, p.52.

21 Ibid., p.55.

22 Sen, Anindya, *Ramakrishna Mission and Community Service in Eastern India - A Qualitative and Quantitative Analysis*, Kolkata, 2005, p.229.

23 *Ibid.*, p.230.

24 *Ibid.*, p.231.

25 *Ibid.*, p.232.

26 Mukherjee, Santana, *Sister Nivedita in Search of Humanity*, p.29.

27 *Ibid.*, p.179.

28 Sen Gupta, Padmini, *The Story of Women of India*, New Delhi, 1974, p.12.

⋐ Chapter 18 ⋑

Vivekananda's Teachings on Religions

Sathya. D

M.Phil in History,
K.M.C.P.G.S, Lawspet,
Puducherry.

"Religion is the idea which is raising the brute unto man and man unto God".[45]

-Swami Vivekananda

Introduction

Vivekananda's teachings stressed on different aspects of religion, education, character building as well as social issues pertaining to India. Among these, *religious* teachings are an important one. For this the best example is the *World's Parliament of Religions* to be held in Chicago in 1893. According to Swami Vivekananda, religion is the idea which is raising the brute into man, and man unto God. He had read the Vedas, the Upanishads, the Gita, and commentaries apart from shastras, puranas and classical Sanskrit literature; and he had

---

45 Swami Lokeswarananda, **"Swami Vivekananda, His Life and Message"**, Kolkatta 1994. P7

also read the scriptures of other religions like Islam, Christianity, Buddhism and Jainism. According to Vivekananda "Buddha is the name of infinite knowledge, infinite as the sky". Vivekananda had good knowledge about the Gita. The book known as the Gita is a part of the Mahabharata. In this he explained the various aspects like, how the name Veda-Vyasa came, and also he raised some of the question regarding the Krishna, etc; Vivekananda was a follower of **Vedanta**, who played a significant role in introducing Vedanta to the Western world. He found practical Vedanta imminent in all religions, either implicitly or explicitly. He preached practical Vedanta and brought into the discussion. Vivekananda also had good knowledge about the Sanniyasa, the final stage of human life. According to Vivekananda, Sanniyasa is "the love of death"; worldly people love life. The sanniyasin is to love death. Through this knowledge, he showed new way to the religion. With this basic idea in mind, the author would like to discuss about Vivekananda's teachings on religion in this chapter.

Swami Vivekananda has been hailed as an awakener of modern India, a national builder, man maker, religious reformer, and synthesizer of science and religion. He had read the Vedas, the Upanishads, the Gita and the commentaries, apart from the shastras, puranas and classical Sanskrit literature; and he also read the scriptures of other religions like Islam, Christianity, Buddhism and Jainism. And he had wandered all over India meeting Pandits and Sadhus in his quest for spiritual knowledge. The fountainhead of Vivekananda's teachings on religion was Sri Ramakrishna, who gave him his insight into real religion, his firm convention about the validity and universality of Vedanta and his equally strong belief in its practical relevance to life and living.[46] More than that, he showed the Indian culture to the world in the World's Parliament of Religion, at Chicago held on 11th September 1893.

Vivekananda's Definition of Religion

Swamiji's definition of religion project his endeavour to make the world realize that the function of religion is fundamentally divine

---

46. V.K.R.V.Rao, "Builders of Modern India Swami Vivekananda," 1990 p143

in character, and that the divinity which is so found within, requires that the life which is lived should be divine in character and divine in all motives. Religion begins with a question, and ends with its answer—"Religion is the manifestation of the Divinity already in man."[47] When a human being realizes the eternal relationship between his self and God, though he/she remains in the world like anyone else, he manifests the highest nature, namely, the Divine. The knowledge of this divinity is the secret of man's development both in individual and collective life, secular as well as spiritual.

India: The land of Religion

The land between the Himalaya and the Vindhyas, the home of the Aryas, the land which gave birth to Krishna and Buddha, the cradle of Great Rajarishis and Brahmarshis, became silent, and from the very furthest end of the Indian Peninsula, from races alien in speech and form, families claiming descent from the ancient Brahmins, came the reaction against the corrupted Buddhism. In the Buddhist movement, the Kshatriyas were the real leaders and whole masses of them became Buddhists. The Kshatriyas have always been backbone of India, they had been supporters of science and liberty. When the greater part of their number sank into ignorance, and another portion mixed their blood with savages from Central Asia and lent their swords to establish the rules of priests in India, her cup became full to the brim, and down sank the land of Bharata. Rajputs have been the glories of ancient India. India can only be raised if the descendants of Kshatriyas co-operate with the descendants of the Brahmins, not to share spoil of pelf and power, but to help the weak, to enlighten the ignorant, and to restore the lost glory of the holy land of their forefathers[48].

Teachings on Vedanta

Vedanta literally means the end of the Vedas. Sometimes in the West, by the Vedas are meant only hymns and rituals. But at the present time

47   Sivaramakrishna. M & Roy Sumita, **"Reflection on Swami Vivekananda Hundred Years after Chicago,"** p65
48   **"Selection from the complete works of Swami Vivekananda "**, Advaida Asharama, New Delhi 2007. Pp 468-470

these parts have almost gone out of use, and usually by the word Vedas, in India, the Vedanta is meant.[49] However, Vedanta takes in not only the truth preached in the Vedas but also the Brahmanas or ritualistic writings; and rest of the Upanishads are independent, not comprised in any of the Brahmanas or other parts of the Vedas; but there is no reason to suppose that they were entirely independent of other parts, for, as we well know, many of these have been lost entirely and many of the Brahmanas have became extinct. So it is quite possible that the independent Upanishads belonged to some Brahmanas, which in course of time fell into discussion, while Upanishads remained. These Upanishads are also called Forest Books of Aranyakas.

The Vedanta, then, practically forms the scriptures of the Hindus, and all systems of philosophy that are orthodox has to take it as their foundation. Even the Buddhists and Jains, when it suits their purpose, will quote a passage from the Vedanta as authority. All schools of philosophy in India, although they claim to have been based upon the Vedas, took different names for their systems. The last one, the system of Vyasa, took its stand upon the doctrine of the Vedas more than the previous systems did, and made an attempt to harmonise the preceding philosophies, such as the Sankhya and Nyaya, with the doctrines of the Vedanta. So it is especially called the Vedanta philosophy; and the Sutras or aphorisms of Vyasa are, in modern India, the basis of Vedanta philosophy. All the Vedantists agree on three points. They believe in God, in the Vedas as revealed, and in Cycles.[50]

Teachings on Hinduism

The Hindus have received their religious revelation through the Vedas. They hold the Vedas are without beginning and without end. It may sound ludicrous to this audience, how a book can be without beginning or end. But by the Vedas no books are meant. They mean the accumulated treasuries of spiritual law discovered by different persons in different times. The discoverers of these laws are called Rishis. The Hindus believe that every soul is a circle whose circumference is nowhere, but mean the change of this centre from body to

49   Ibid., p 82
50   Swami Vivekananda, **"Vedanta philosophy"**. Advaita Ashrama, Kolkata.2008 Pp 13-18

body. Nor is the soul bound by the conditions of matter. In its very essence, it is free, unbounded, holy, pure, and thinks of itself as matter. The Hindus have associated the ideas of holiness, purity, truth, omnipresence, and such other ideas with different images and forms. To the Hindu, man is not travelling from error to truth, but from truth to truth, from lower to higher truth. Unity in variety is the plan of nature, and the Hindu has recognized. Every other religion lays down certain fixed dogmas, and tries to force society to adopt them. The Hindus have discovered that the absolute can only be realized, or thought of, or stated, through the relatives, and the images, crosses and crescents are simply so many symbols, so many pegs to hang the spiritual ideas on. It is not that this help is necessary for everyone, but for those that it is wrong. Nor is it compulsory in Hinduism.[51]

Teachings on Gita

The book known as the Gita forms a part of the Mahabharata. Vivekananda says that, to understand the Gita properly several things are very important to know. First, whether it formed a part of the Mahabharata, that is, whether authorship attributed to Veda-Vyasa was true, or if it merely interpolated within the great epic; secondly, whether there was any historical personality of the name of Krishna; thirdly, whether the great war of Kurukshetra as mentioned in the Gita actually took place; and fourthly, whether Arjuna and others were real historical persons. Where in lies the originality of the Gita, which distinguished it from all preceding scriptures? It is this: though before its advent, Yoga, Jnana, Bhakti, etc., had each its strong adherents, they all quarreled among themselves, each claiming superiority for his own chosen path; no one ever tried to seek for reconciliation among these different paths. It was the author of the Gita who for the first time tried to harmonise these. He took the best from what all the sects then existing had to offer, and threaded them in the Gita, but even where Krishna failed to show a complete reconciliation[52].

---

51   Swami Lokeswarananda, **"Swami Vivekananda: His Life and Message"**, Kolkata 1994. Pp 64-69
52   A Class-talk given at the Alambazar Math in 1897-- **"Selection from The complete works of Swami Vivekananda"**, Advaida Asharama, New Delhi 2007. Pp 367-370

Lord Buddha and Buddhism

Buddhism is one of our sects. It was founded by a great man called Gautama, who became disgusted with the eternal metaphysical discussions of his day, and the cumbrous rituals and more especially with the caste system. According to Vivekananda, "Buddha is the name of infinite knowledge, infinite as the sky". Buddha did not want to go to heaven, did not want money; he gave up throne and everything else, and he went about begging his bread through the streets of India, preaching for the good of men and animals with a heart as wide as the ocean. He was the only man who was ever ready to give up his life for animal sacrifice. Buddha once said to a king, "If the sacrifices of a lamb help you to go to heaven, sacrificing of a man will help you better, and so sacrifice me." The king was astonished. Too many paths become easier if they believe in God. But the life of Buddha shows that even a man who does not believe in God, has no metaphysics, does not belong to any sect, and does not go to any church, or temple, and is a confessed materialist, even he can attain the highest. Buddha may or may not have believed in God; that does not matter. Buddha reached the state of perfection to which others come by Bhakti, i.e., love of God, Yoga, or Jnana. Perfection does not come from belief or faith. Perfection comes through the disinterested performance of action.[53]

Quran and Islamism

During this time, India had two major religions (Hinduism and Islamism). Vivekananda taught not only Hinduism but also about Quran and Islamism. Vivekananda wrote the unity of two major religions of India. The practical Advaitism which looks upon and behaves towards all mankind as 'one' soul, is yet to be developed among the Hindu universally...firmly persuaded that without the help of practical Islam, the theories of Vedantism, however fine and wonderful they may be, are entirely valueless to the vast mass of mankind. We want to lead mankind to the place where there is neither the Vedas, the Bible nor the Quran: yet this has to be done by harmonising the Vedas, the Bible and the Quran. Mankind ought to be taught that religions are the varied expressions of the Religion which is Oneness,

53   Ibid., Swami Vivekananda Delivered in Detroit- pp 361-362

so that each may choose the path that suits him best. For our own motherland, a junction of the two great systems—Hinduism and Islam, i.e., Vedantic brain and Islamic body—is the only hope.[54]

Christ the Messenger

The vibration of light is everywhere, omnipresent, but we have to strike the light of the lamp before we can see the light. The omnipresent God of the universe cannot be seen until He is reflected by these giant lamps of the earth—the prophets, the man-God, the Incarnations, the embodiments of God. That God is Christ the Messenger. When Christ was born, the Jews were in the state. The Jewish race found its expression at the next period, in the rise of Christianity. The gathered streams joined together, and became surging wave on the top of which we find standing out the character, a Jesus of Nazareth. Thus, every Prophet is a creation of his races; Jesus, himself creator of the future. The cause of today is the effect of the past and cause for the future. In this position stands the Messenger. The voice of Asia has been the voice of religion. The voice of Europe is the voice of Ancient Greece. Whatever the Greeks do is right and correct. The Greek live entirely in this world. And the Greek being the teachers of all subsequent Europeanism, the voice of the Europe is Greek.

There is another type in Asia. Think of that vast, huge continent, whose mountain-tops go beyond the clouds, almost touching the canopy of heaven's blue; a rolling desert of miles upon miles. Where a drop of water cannot be found, neither will a blade of grass grow; there is also the thirst for Nature, and there is also the same thirst for power; there is also the same thirst for excellence, the same idea of Greek and Barbarian; but it has extended over a larger circle. In Asia, even today, birth or colour or languages never make a race. That which makes a race is its religion. "We are all Christians; we are all Mohammedans; we are all Hindus, or all Buddhist.[55] Religion is the tie, the unity of humanity. And then again. The Oriental, for the

---

54 Sivaramakrishna.M & Roy Sumita, **"Reflection on Swami Vivekananda Hundred Years after Chicago" p 82**

55   A lecture delivered at Los Angeles, California, 1990-- **"Selection from The complete works of Swami Vivekananda",** Advaita Asharama, New Delhi 2007. P 324

same reason, is visionary, is a born dreamer. The Orient has been the cradle of the human race for ages. Jesus of Nazareth, in the first place, the rue son of the Orient, intensely practical".[56]

One Planet one People

Vivekananda expressed confidence that if such a religion was offered, all nations would follow it. During his travels in America, he called for a cooperative effort in educating and helping the multitudes of India in establishing a society on the pattern of Western democracies but permeated by the spirit of the Vedanta so that India could realize her spiritual destiny and contribute to world peace and brotherhood. He advocated the compositeness of the Indian culture stating,

"Aryan, Dravidian, Tartar, Turkish, Mughal, European—it's as if the blood of all nations flows in this country. There is marvelous mélange of many languages and in customs and practice there is often more variety between two Indian sub-nationalities than between Europe and the East... Harmonisation of different religions is the first item in the agenda of building a future India."

The message of Swami Vivekananda was chiefly designed to set a new direction and lend a fresh impulse to the elevation of the spiritually impoverished, colonially dominated, case-ridden society. A new and much higher level of consciousness is indispensable to India's proper understanding of the eternal values of religion as rediscovered.[57]

Other Teachings on Religions

There are four general types of men—the rational, the emotional, the mystical and the worker. For each, there must be a suitable form of worship. The ultimate goal of all mankind, the aim and end of all religions, is but one—reunion with God. The goal and methods are employed through Yoga. There are various such Yogas or methods of union—but the chief ones are:

56   Ibid pp 320-325
57   Sivaramakrishna.M & Roy Sumita, "Reflection on Swami Vivekananda Hundred Years after Chicago" p81

1. Karma Yoga—the manner in which a man realizes his own divinity through works and duty.

2. Bhakti Yoga—the Realization of the divinity through devotion to, and love of, a personal God.

3. Raja Yoga—the Realization of the divinity through the control of mind.

4. Jnana Yoga—the Realization of a man's own divinity through knowledge.[58]

Vivekananda also taught about Bhakti, spirituality, and sannyasa in the detailed manner.

Conclusion

The essence of Vivekananda's teachings on religion was the universality of God and his accessibility both from within and out, the divinity of man, respect and understanding of all religions, the equality and brotherhood of men, the supreme virtue of compassion, work without attachment, devotion without return, renunciation of the personal ego, and service of all men and especially of those who were poor or maimed or illiterate or disinherited, the daridranarayanas of this world. To Vivekananda, religion was not just a question of belief. "Religion", he said "was realization, not talk, not doctrine, not theories however beautiful they may be: It is being and becoming; not hearing and acknowledging". According to Sister Nivedita, his Irish disciple, Vivekananda had a two-fold mission: 'nation-making' and 'world-moving'.[59] Vivekananda's teachings on religion was mainly focused to open the eyes of the Indian people; not only to open the eyes of Indian people, but also the 19th century world, to turn towards Indian culture and Indian religion. This was made possible because of Swami Vivekananda and his teachings on religions.

REFERENCES

58 Swami Lokeswarananda, **"Swami Vivekananda: His Life and Message"**, Kolkata 1994 pp9-10
59 Ibid.,p 39

1. Selection from the Complete Works of Swami Vivekananda, By Advaita Ashrama, Printed in India at Swapna Printing Works, Kolkatta. 2007

2. Reflection on Swami Vivekananda, (Hundered Years After Chicago), Edited by Sivaramakrishna.M and Roy Sumita,Sterling Publishers Private Limited, New Delhi.1993

3. 19th century thought in Bengal, Edited by Kalyan Sengupta and Tirthanath Bandyopadhyay, Allied Publishers Limited,Calcutta.1998

4. Builders of Modern India Swami Vivekananda, V.K.R.V.Rao, Publication Division Ministry of Information and Broadcasting, Government of India, New Delhi.1990

5. Swami Vivekananda: His Life and Message, Compiled and Edited by Swami Lokeswarananda, Printed in India - Ramakrishna Mission Institute of Culture, Kolkata.1992

6. Vedanta Philosophy by Swami Vivekananda Published by Advaita Ashrama, Kolkata. 2008

7. The Science and Philosophy of Religion by Swami Vivekananda Printed In Advaita Ashrama, Kolkata.2009

8. History and Philosophy of Swami Vivekananda, published by Ramakrishna Mission Institute of Culture, Mylapore, Chennai. 2011

9. Life of Swami Vivekananda By Eastern and Western Disciples, Advaita Ashrama, Calcutta (1992)

10. Swami Vivekananda-Awakener of Modern India by R.Ramakrishnan, published by Ramakrishna Math, Mylapore, Madras (1964)

~ Index ~

Europe 21, 41, 104, 122, 177, 178

European 41, 65, 98, 147, 178

European Countries 65, 147

Exclusivism 5

Ezhava 57

F

Female Infanticide 155

G

Gandhiji 25, 38, 43, 60, 104

Geography 165, 166

Geometry 165

German Emperor 23

Gita 16, 33, 65, 92, 150, 171, 172, 175

Gurukula 60, 69, 119, 130

H

Harijan 55, 56, 60-62

Harijan Poojaris 55

Haripad 54, 58, 59, 66

Himalaya 173

Himalayas 20, 91

Hindu Dharma 10, 93

Hinduism 13, 14, 21, 22, 37, 40, 47-49, 95, 97, 99, 151, 152, 174-177

Hindu Marriage 108

Hindu Napoleon 37

Hindu Philosophy 47

Hindus 15, 46, 47, 92, 93, 95, 97, 99, 153, 174, 175, 177

History 1, 9, 19, 36, 45, 53, 67, 71, 74, 77, 91, 101, 103, 113, 145, 154-156, 165, 166, 168, 171, 180

Hyderabad 9, 124, 143

I

Inclusivism 5

Indian Culture 10, 31, 110, 121, 134, 172, 178, 179

Indian Unrest 126

Indira Gandhi Award for National Integration 65

Iran 65

Islam 65, 172, 176, 177

Ittirappa Menon 56

Izhavas 50

J

Jaffna University 21, 23

Jainism 172

Jains 15, 174

Jawaharlal Nehru 50, 137

Jesus 12, 14-17, 24, 177, 178

Jews 1, 109, 177

Jhelum 108

Jnana 11, 63, 95, 175, 176, 179

Jnana Yoga 63

John Stuart Mill 73

Judaism 14

K

Kaduvelicittar 146

Kakapusundar 149

Kalady 55, 57, 61, 63, 66

Kaloor 56

Karachi 65